NEWS OF F

ncis Henry Durbridge was born in Hull, Yorkshire, in 1912 and was educated at Bradford Grammar School. He was encouraged at an early age to write by his English teacher and went on to read English at Birmingham University. At the age of twenty one he sold a play to the BBC and continued to write following his graduation whilst working as a stockbroker's clerk.

In 1938, he created the character Paul Temple, a crime novelist and detective. Many others followed and they were hugely successful until the last of the series was completed in 1968. In 1969, the Paul Temple series was adapted for television and four of the adventures prior to this, had been adapted for cinema, albeit with less success than radio and TV. Francis Durbridge also wrote for the stage and continued doing so up until 1991, when *Sweet Revenge* was completed. Additionally, he wrote over twenty other well received novels, most of which were on the general subject of crime. The last, *Fatal Encounter*, was published after his death in 1998.

Also in this series

FRANCIS DURBRIDGE

News of Paul Temple

COLLINS
CRIME
CLUB

COLLINS CRIME CLUB

An imprint of HarperCollins*Publishers*
1 London Bridge Street
London SE1 9GF
www.harpercollins.co.uk

This paperback edition 2015

First published in Great Britain by
LONG 1940

A catalogue record for this book is
available from the British Library

ISBN 978-0-00-812560-8

Set in Sabon by FMG using Atomik ePublisher from Easypress

MIX
Paper from
responsible sources
FSC
www.fsc.org FSC C007454

CHAPTER I

The Stage is Set

1

'Bryant! Where the devil is Bryant?' Ralph Cosgrove, news editor of the *Evening Post*, replaced the telephone and repeated his question into the mouthpiece of the dictograph. A few seconds later the door opened and a resonant tenor announced: 'Do I hear you calling me?'

'Cut out the fooling and shut the door,' snapped Cosgrove. 'You should have been here hours ago. What the devil have you been doing?'

Rex Bryant came into the office and perched himself on the arm of the chair reserved for visitors. He was young, attractive, well dressed, and, oddly enough, did *not* wear a trilby on the back of his head. 'I've been to a movie,' announced Rex. 'It was terrific. All about a newspaper. The editor got the scoop. The reporter got the girl. And the girl got the baby.'

There was an unpleasant glint in Cosgrove's eye. 'Unless you take the lead out of your pants you'll get the sack!' he barked.

1

'Get down to Southampton and cover the *Clipper* story!'

Rex frowned. 'Look here, Chief, I'm just about tired of meeting film stars.'

'I'm not asking you to meet film stars. Maybe you've never heard of the *Golden Clipper*?'

'Of course I have! New York to Southampton in twenty-four hours. Nice easy passage. Where's the story?'

Ralph Cosgrove smiled. It was not a pleasant smile. 'I don't suppose you know by any chance who happens to be travelling on the *Clipper*?'

'The Quintuplets?' suggested Rex.

Cosgrove thoughtfully fingered a newspaper cutting he had picked up from among the pile of papers on his desk.

'No, not the Quintuplets,' he said softly. 'Just Paul Temple. Mr and Mrs Temple, to be more precise.'

'Are you sure of this?' There was no mistaking the note of urgency in Rex Bryant's voice.

'Of course I'm sure. It was in last night's *Standard*.'

'Well, I'm damned!'

'You'll also be fired if you don't get down to Southampton. We've been waiting for this story to break for weeks.'

'But everybody knows why Temple is on his way home,' protested Rex. 'They've been rehearsing that new play of his. It's due to open in a fortnight.'

'That's old stuff. Iris Archer in *The First Lady Seaton*.'

'Yes. Only for some reason or other Iris Archer isn't going to play the part.'

This was obviously news to Cosgrove and he raised his eyebrows in surprise. 'What's the matter with Archer? Why isn't she playing the part?'

'I don't know. Gibson had a chat with her last night. She talks a lot of nonsense about the part being unsuitable.'

Cosgrove nodded. 'Well, get down to Southampton and see what Temple has to say about it.'

Rex wearily levered himself from the arm of the chair.

'I'd sooner cover that new movie at the Empire,' he grinned. 'It's all about an editor who took the wrong turning.'

'Southampton!'

'OK, Snow White! OK!'

Rex made a hasty yet dignified retreat.

Four hours later, his vermilion two-seater sports car was nosing its way through Southampton's dock traffic, and he was wondering if there would be any other newspapermen present. There was nothing Rex hated more than mass interviews. However, knowing Temple and his wife in the days when they were both journalists was certainly a point in his favour. When the *Golden Clipper* bumped gently to a standstill, Rex had no difficulty in segregating Paul Temple and Steve from the crowds that thronged to see Hollywood's latest film face, which, as usual, proved more than a little disappointing in its everyday proportions.

Over a drink in the buffet, Rex surveyed his old acquaintances with a quizzical stare. Temple, he decided, had hardly altered as far as features were concerned since the days when he was a penurious journalist. True, he must be quite a stone lighter, but that suited him.

Steve, who was always ready to talk 'shop' with Bryant or any of the other reporters, said quietly: 'How's the circulation, Rex?'

'Not so good lately. Wrong time of year.'

'It's always the wrong time of year,' put in Temple, with a twinkle in his eye.

'They're sending us out after all sorts of stories that the subs slaughter down to four lines on page eight,' declared Rex moodily, ordering himself another whisky.

3

'What exactly are you doing down at Southampton?' demanded Steve curiously.

Rex splashed soda into his glass. 'To be quite candid, I came down here to see your delightful husband,' he grinned.

'Things must certainly be in a bad way if I'm considered to be in the news,' laughed Temple. 'What's it all about?'

Rex took a cigarette from his case and scratched a match. 'The play, for one thing. You might as well give me all the dope about it. Be a sport, Temple – it isn't as if the publicity will do the show any harm – or will it?'

'By Timothy, you boys must be hard up for news,' murmured Temple sympathetically.

'There isn't any story, Rex,' added Steve wistfully. 'If there was a story, you could have it like a shot, couldn't he, darling?'

Temple nodded. 'Like a shot,' he corroborated.

'But is Iris Archer leaving the cast, or isn't she?'

Temple dived in his pocket and produced a crumpled Western Union Cable. 'I got this just before we left New York; that's all I know.' He tossed the cable over to the reporter, who straightened it out and read:

Terribly sorry unable to play Lady Seaton stop will explain later stop lots of love Iris.

'And a very large full stop,' added Temple ruefully.

Rex folded the paper and handed it back to the novelist. 'I thought you wrote the play specially for Iris Archer.'

'So I did.'

Rex wrinkled his forehead. 'Then it seems funny that—'

'Don't worry him, Rex,' advised Steve, who knew just how sore the point was with her husband.

'But look here, I've got to have some sort of a story to take back to town!'

Temple and Steve regarded him innocently.

'Hadn't you better go and catch Sylvia Larone before she gets the train?' suggested Steve. 'You could ask her what she really thought of Hollywood.'

Rex ignored the suggestion. 'Tell me your plans for the future,' he said.

'We're going to Scotland for three weeks.'

'The South of France, dear,' Steve prompted gently.

'Scotland,' repeated Temple firmly.

'The South of France.'

'All right,' chipped in Rex, eyeing them impatiently. 'I'll say Scotland *and* the South of France. Then what?'

Temple said quietly: 'Well, I've promised my publishers a new novel for Christmas—'

Rex shifted impatiently on his high stool.

'I'm not running the literary page,' he said heavily. 'I've got to go back to town with a story. Not a "puff" for a new novel.'

'But we haven't got a story, Rex. Nothing's happened – nothing at all.'

Rex shook his head sadly. 'All right,' he murmured resignedly. 'Tell me something about the trip – your personal reactions and all that sort of hot air. I'll have to turn in a couple of "sticks" or they'll murder me.'

Temple laughed. Then he caught sight of a distinguished-looking man who had just entered the buffet.

'Here's Doctor Steiner. He'll tell you all about the trip – won't you, Doctor?'

Temple introduced the newcomer.

'It will be possible to get a train soon, Mr Temple?' queried the doctor.

'Why yes – it's due almost any minute. Then I'm afraid we shall have to leave you. We go by road,' said Temple.

'Ach, it is sad to part so soon. It has been such a pleasant journey and a wonderful experience. Just look at my buttonhole – the carnation is quite fresh, and I bought it in New York.'

Rex Bryant was impressed with this small point. The doctor was obviously a man who noticed things.

'Perhaps you wouldn't mind giving me a sort of interview, sir,' he barged in hastily. 'Is this your first trip across the Atlantic?'

'I should have warned you, Doctor, that Mr Bryant is a representative of the London *Evening Post*. One of our most respected publications,' Temple added with a twinkle.

'So,' grunted Steiner. 'A reporter? This England becomes more like New York every day. No, young man, this is not my first trip – I have been many times before.'

'Have you any intention of visiting the other European countries, Doctor?' asked Rex.

'I do not know, my friend. That I shall decide later.'

'H'm,' murmured Rex thoughtfully, taking a grubby envelope and pencil from his inside pocket. 'I didn't quite get your name, sir?'

'The name is Steiner,' said the German in dignified tones. 'Doctor Ludwig Steiner. Professor of Philosophy at the University of Philadelphia.'

'What's your interest in coming to Europe, Doctor?' Rex paused significantly. 'Have you an interest in politics or . . . ?'

The doctor shook his head. 'I am over here on holiday, my friend,' he said. Then added as an afterthought: 'Just a holiday.'

2

There was something both distinctive and rather strange about Iris Archer's well-moulded features, smooth fair hair, limpid blue eyes and vibrating voice. 'She's always Iris Archer,' her critics commented, and to some extent this criticism was justified, but they rather forgot that Iris owed her success to the fact that she was able to shape an indifferent part to her own individual personality. There was something mysterious, glamorous, and rather different about Iris Archer. Seeing her on the stage one could not help feeling that she led an exciting life, that some tall, distinguished young man (hair slightly grey at the temples) was perpetually in her dressing room waiting to take her to the Savoy grill.

Iris had suddenly appeared in the West End. Some said she had played small parts on Broadway, others declared that she had toured in an obscure concert party and had inherited a sum of money with which she had set herself up in London. Certainly her very early days were never mentioned in any interview, no matter how persistent the gossip writer became.

Though she always contrived to give her acquaintances the impression that she could afford very little time to trouble about clothes, Iris was always dressed in a simple but striking fashion that lingered just a shade too long in the masculine memory.

Paul Temple had been rather surprised to meet her at a cocktail party given by a comparatively unknown publisher. Temple was even more surprised to discover that she could discuss all the latest best-sellers with an intelligence that betokened not only wide reading but a very close observation of the many spheres of life.

And what had impressed him most of all was the fact that she had not begged him to write a play for her. Nevertheless, Temple had returned home determined to do so. *The First Lady Seaton* was the result. It had been shelved for over a year in view of other commitments, for Temple was determined that none but Iris Archer should play the leading part.

'Lady Seaton' was a queer and unusual character. Temple felt certain that, played by anyone but Iris, it would prove unsympathetic. Iris had just those qualities to bring 'Lady Seaton' to life; to make her a distinctive creation unlike any other heroine he could ever remember seeing on the English stage.

He had been more than a little taken aback by her cable and was still deeply puzzled by it. Nevertheless, they had been in their Mayfair flat for several days before Iris made her customary extravagant entrance.

'Darling, how nice to see you again!' As always, there was just the right inflection in Iris' voice.

Paul Temple and Steve rose to welcome her.

'Steve, my dear, you look marvellous!' cried Iris, holding out both hands. 'Doesn't she look marvellous, Paul? Now do tell me about the trip, I'm simply dying to hear all about it. Did you feel frightened?'

'A little,' confessed Steve, who was not very much at home in the air.

'My dear, I should have been petrified,' said Iris. 'The very thought of all that water makes me positively violent.'

She seated herself with a tiny sigh of content.

'You look very fit, Iris,' said Temple quietly, surveying her intently.

'I'm not, darling. Feel awful at times.'

'Won't you take your things off, Iris?' suggested Steve.

Iris smiled and nervously fingered the clasp of her fox cape.

'No, I can't stay very long, darling.'

'What about a cocktail?' suggested Temple.

'Yes,' decided Iris after a short pause. 'Yes, I would rather like a drink, my sweet.'

Temple went across to the cocktail cabinet and consulted a slip on which a recipe was typed. He remembered that Iris had a favourite cocktail.

'Paul, you got my cable?' Iris asked presently.

'Yes,' replied Temple, 'it was handed to me just as we were getting on the 'plane.'

'Were you surprised?'

Temple carefully speared a cherry before answering.

'Well, just a little.' There was an awkward pause. 'Iris, are you serious about this?'

'I don't think I've ever been quite so serious in my life before,' said Iris grimly.

'But why?' cried Steve in obvious surprise. 'What's the matter? Has Seaman been nasty about something?' It was quite obvious that Steve was as anxious about the play as Temple himself.

'No, no, it's not that. He's a swell producer,' replied Iris hastily.

'Is it money?' asked Temple rather tentatively. 'I thought we'd offered you a splendid contract. After all, we gave way to you over that picture business.'

Iris was somewhat at a loss for words.

'I've been badly miscast, Paul,' she said at last, but her tone was strangely unconvincing.

Temple could not help laughing.

'But that's ridiculous! You said yourself the part fitted you like a glove.'

Iris nodded. 'That was six weeks ago,' she added quietly. There was a disturbing note in her voice.

'Aren't you very well, Iris?' queried Temple rather anxiously.

'Not terribly,' she confessed.

'What are you going to do? Make a film?'

'No,' replied Iris uncertainly. 'I'm—well, I'm going to the South of France for two months. When I get back I may start work again—I don't know—yet . . .'

9

'Are you going alone?'

'Yes, quite alone. To a small place near St Maxime.'

Temple shrugged his shoulders and handed Iris her cocktail.

'Well, I'm sorry about all this,' he said, and forced a smile. 'I suppose it can't be helped.'

'You're very sweet about it,' smiled Iris, her limpid blue eyes suddenly warm and friendly.

'I suppose there *isn't* a chance that you might change your mind about the play?'

Iris shook her head regretfully. 'No. No, I'm afraid there isn't, darling.'

'Iris, do you mind if I tell you something quite frankly?' said Temple suddenly. 'Six months ago you wrote me a letter about the play. You said you thought it was well written, extremely amusing, and that the part of "Lady Seaton" was quite the best part offered you for many years.'

'Oh yes, I did,' agreed Iris flippantly. 'I remember the letter perfectly. And I meant it, Paul. Every word of it.' She leaned forward. 'Really, I was quite sincere.'

'Yes,' smiled Temple. 'Yes, I know you were.'

Temple felt it was high time the cards went on the table. 'Iris, why are you leaving the cast?' he demanded flatly. 'It's not because you don't like the play any longer. I know you well enough to realise you wouldn't change your mind. It's not because the part doesn't suit you. You've got another and more important reason, haven't you?'

It was some little time before Iris spoke, but when she did there was a strange and somewhat urgent note in her voice.

'Yes,' she admitted. 'But it's no use asking me what that reason is, because I can't tell you.'

Temple rose and poured himself a drink.

'If we postponed the production, say for two or three months,' he suggested, 'would that be all right?'

Iris looked a little bewildered. 'You mean, would I be prepared to play "Lady Seaton" if you held things over, till . . . say, just before Christmas?'

Temple nodded.

'But darling, you can't do that!'

'You haven't answered my question,' he persisted.

Iris took a cigarette from her case. 'I should love to do it, Paul,' she said softly. 'It's a fine play, and a wonderful part for me, but—'

'But what?'

'But I must be free between now and the tenth of November.'

Temple perched himself on the arm of a chair and looked into her eyes. 'All right, then that's settled,' he said. 'I'll write to Seaman tonight.'

'Paul, you're a darling!' cried Iris in amazement. 'The thought of not playing "Lady Seaton" nearly broke my heart.' She was obviously both genuinely relieved and delighted.

'Go ahead and kiss him, Iris!' smiled Steve. 'It's overrated, anyway.'

'You don't know what a weight you've taken off my mind, Paul,' said Iris, finishing her cocktail. 'Now, I really must fly!'

'When are you leaving?' asked Steve.

'On Saturday – by 'plane at midday.'

'And I can tell Seaman you'll be back in town for the end of November!' pursued Temple.

'Not a day later than the seventeenth, I promise you,' replied Iris, drawing on her gloves.

'Good. Then take care of yourself, Iris,' laughed Temple. 'I don't want any accidents happening to my leading lady.'

11

Iris was turning to go when Temple's manservant opened the door and announced Sir Graham Forbes.

Both Temple and his wife appeared surprised, for they had not seen Sir Graham for some months. Steve was more than a little alarmed, for Sir Graham's visits were usually associated with something a little more exciting than afternoon tea.

'It's all right, Steve,' smiled her husband, 'there's nothing to get excited about.'

'Sir Graham Forbes?' queried Iris, setting her hat at a jaunty angle. 'Isn't he connected with Scotland Yard or something?'

'It is Scotland Yard,' Temple informed her, as she followed Pryce. She bade them an extravagant farewell, and Temple once more repeated his assurance that he would write to Seaman that night.

As Pryce carefully closed the door, Steve turned to her husband with a worried frown. 'Paul, if Sir Graham is here because he needs your help, then please—' There was a catch in her voice.

Temple squeezed her arm affectionately.

'Sir Graham is here because he needs a cocktail. A very strong cocktail. And nothing else, Mrs Temple,' came the urbane voice of Scotland Yard's Chief Commissioner.

'Why, Sir Graham!' ejaculated Steve.

'Come along in, Sir Graham!' laughed Temple. 'It's grand seeing you again. Though I thought Pryce—'

'Yes, Pryce wanted to announce me all right,' smiled Sir Graham. 'But he seemed to have his hands full with the blonde.'

'That was Iris Archer. You've probably heard of her,' Temple informed him.

'Iris Archer?' Sir Graham was obviously impressed.

Temple crossed over to the cocktail cabinet.

'What would you like, Sir Graham? Sherry? Bronx?'

'I'd rather like a Bronx,' said Sir Graham, watching Temple rather curiously as he selected the ingredients. 'What was the trip like, Temple? Got a bit of a shock when I heard you were coming over on the *Clipper*.'

'Oh, lovely!' enthused Steve. 'We enjoyed every minute of it, didn't we, darling?'

'Every minute,' agreed Temple, handing their visitor his drink and then pouring out a glass of sherry for Steve.

Sir Graham smacked his lips.

'Isn't Iris Archer going into a play of yours? I seem to remember reading something about it?' he asked.

'Well, she *was* going into a play of mine,' replied Temple. 'Now things seem a little uncertain.'

'H'm. Pity.' grunted Forbes, who understood little or nothing of the complications that arise in the theatre world.

'What's Scotland Yard doing at the moment?' asked Temple.

'Just at the moment,' began Forbes with elaborate emphasis, 'we are up against one of the greatest criminal organisations—'

Steve had almost risen from her chair, and Sir Graham broke into a heavy laugh.

'He's only pulling your leg, darling,' Temple reassured her, but somehow Steve did not altogether appreciate the joke.

'As a matter of fact, things are pretty dead. They have been for months,' continued the Chief Commissioner evenly. 'One or two isolated murders, but nothing really big since "The Front Page Men", and I can't honestly say I'm sorry.' He drained his glass and got up.

'I must be on my way – I only dropped in to welcome the wanderers home again.'

'We're going away again in a day or two,' said Temple, 'but when we get back you must come to dinner and—'

'I shall be out of town myself for about a month,' broke in Sir Graham. 'First holiday I've taken for nearly six years.'

Temple said casually: 'Where are you going?'

'Carol's taken a villa just outside Nice.'

'Nice!' echoed Steve in some surprise.

'Yes,' said Forbes. 'I say, you two don't happen to be going to the South of France, by any chance?'

'Oddly enough, Sir Graham—' began Temple.

'We're going to Scotland,' finished Steve. 'You did want to go to Scotland, didn't you, darling?'

'Why—er—yes. Yes, of course,' said Temple in some embarrassment.

'Then that's fine,' smiled Steve, rather delighted by her husband's unexpected confusion.

'Well, wherever you go, Temple, keep out of mischief,' said Forbes.

Steve smiled. It was a very pleasant smile.

'That's just why we are going to Scotland!' she said.

3

For five hours Temple had been driving steadily through variable Scottish weather. They had stopped at Dunfermline to gaze open-mouthed upon the many evidences of the benevolence of Mr Andrew Carnegie. They had even paused some time at the tomb of Robert the Bruce, and, rather to Steve's amusement, Temple had drawn many parallels between the tenacity of that legendary figure and the patience required in the solution of modern crime mysteries.

As they continued their journey towards Inverdale, where they proposed to spend a few days, the sky suddenly darkened, and on a particularly lonely stretch of moorland the rain lashed furiously against the windscreen.

Steve was never very comfortable during thunderstorms, and when the sky was streaked with forked flashes she begged her husband to stop. But Temple drove on, holding the theory that a moving vehicle is a less likely target for lightning.

'The rain seems to be getting worse,' shouted Steve above the noise of the storm. Temple, struggling with the windscreen wiper, which was sticking occasionally, muttered an imprecation.

'I don't believe the lightning is quite so bad now,' added Steve, after a pause.

'Perhaps not,' replied Temple, who had not been paying much attention to it. 'This road is terrible. If we get a puncture now, everything in the garden will be lovely!'

'I wonder how many miles we are from Inverdale,' Steve speculated, eyeing a range of mountains which seemed deceptively near.

'I'm beginning to wonder if there is such a place,' grunted Temple.

'There must be, darling. It's on the map.'

'That's a very old map,' Temple pointed out as he stepped on the footbrake. 'Hallo, what's this?'

'This' was a cluster of about twenty cottages, scattered at varying intervals along the road.

'Looks like a village of some sort,' said Steve, as the car approached.

'"Some sort" is about right,' grimaced Temple. 'I hope this isn't Inverdale.'

'It can't be, darling. There's nothing except cottages.'

A solitary cow was straying homewards, and Temple had to slow the car down to practically walking pace. The storm had almost passed over by now, and Temple was anxious to find a signpost of some description. 'It's no good going on if we're off the right road,' he told Steve, who was busy unfolding the map. He stopped the car outside the first of the cottages.

Temple glanced at the clock on the dashboard. It was only half-past six. Steve was busy tracing the route they had followed. 'We must have done nearly two hundred miles,' she estimated.

Her husband, who had been surveying the rather unprepossessing cottages, suddenly announced: 'That second cottage is a shop by the look of things. They'd put us on the right track.'

'Yes, perhaps it would be quicker,' agreed Steve. 'Get me some chocolate, darling – fruit and nut.'

'You wouldn't like a juicy steak, by any chance, with *sauté* potatoes?' suggested Temple as he climbed out of the car.

'What, no onions!' Steve riposted, and the novelist laughed.

Temple approached the cottage, which differed from the others in that it had a roof of slates, and its greystone walls bore no trace of whitewash. He pushed open the heavy door, and a tiny bell clanged discordantly. The interior was gloomy and cluttered with a miscellany of articles ranging from flypapers to sides of bacon suspended from the ceiling.

A tight-lipped Scotswoman in her late forties came into the shop from the kitchen. She had a voice that droned rather than spoke and she eyed Temple with obvious suspicion.

'What can I get ye?' she demanded in reply to Temple's civil greeting.

'I should like some chocolate, please.'

'We don't keep chocolate.'

'Oh, I see,' murmured Temple, rather taken aback. 'Very well, I'll have some postcards.'

'A packet?'

'Yes – a packet,' agreed Temple, regarding them rather dubiously.

'Six delightful views of Inverdale,' announced the woman. 'Two by moonlight. That'll be sixpence.'

Temple produced a coin.

'I'll put them in an envelope for ye,' offered the woman rather surprisingly, opening a drawer at the back of the counter.

'How far is Inverdale from here?' asked Temple politely.

'About two miles.'

'Oh, good. I thought it was farther than that.'

'No,' intoned the woman. 'Two miles.' She threw Temple's sixpence into the drawer and closed it sharply.

'I suppose there's some sort of an hotel at Inverdale?'

The woman appeared to be searching her memory. 'Yes,' she decided at last. 'There's an inn.'

'A good one?'

'Not bad—it's not at all bad.'

'Do I keep straight on from here, or is there a turning before—'

He broke off in some embarrassment before the piercing glance from the steely grey eyes.

'Ye're a stranger round these parts?' she observed coldly.

'Very much so, I'm afraid,' he tried to answer in an easy tone.

'Have ye come far?'

This is practically a cross-examination, reflected Temple. But he said: 'London.'

'London? That's a long way,' commented the woman, in a rather warmer tone. 'I've a married sister in London. Peckham, I think it is. Would there be a place called Peckham?'

Temple nodded. 'Yes,' he said, 'there is a place called Peckham.'

'It must be a wonderful thing to travel,' sighed the woman. 'Often wish I had the time, an' money o' course. What was it Shakespeare said about travellers?'

'As far as I can gather, he said quite a number of things,' smiled Temple.

'H'm—will ye be wanting anything else now?' Her voice was cold, almost as if she regretted the previous conversation.

Temple was about to reply when the doorbell clanged violently and a very excited young man entered the shop. He had obviously been running hard, for he stood against the door with almost a sigh of relief.

'Why, Mr Lindsay!' exclaimed the woman in some surprise.

'Hello, Mrs Moffat,' gasped Lindsay.

'Gracious me, ye've certainly been running!'

'I'm sorry for bursting in like this,' he apologised. 'No, please don't go, sir!' There was a note of urgency in his voice as he placed his hand on Temple's sleeve. In another minute he had recovered his breath.

'Apart from being out of breath, you seem rather excited about something,' said Temple. 'Is anything the matter?'

David Lindsay smiled. It was a very infectious smile.

'I saw your car about a quarter of a mile back. Then I saw you stop at Mrs Moffat's, so I raced along after you. I was afraid you might get started again before . . . before I could get here in time.'

'Can I help you at all?' queried Temple, who rather liked the look of the young man.

'I was wondering if you happened to be going to Inverdale?'

'Yes, as a matter of fact I am.'

'Then would you be good enough to do me a favour?'

'Well, I might. What is it exactly?'

'There's an inn at Inverdale,' said Lindsay, 'called the "Royal Gate". I don't know whether you know it or not?'

'As a matter of fact my wife and I intend spending the night at Inverdale, so—'

'Oh, that's splendid!' Lindsay's blue eyes lit up. 'Well, when you get there, would you be good enough to ask for a Mr John Richmond, and then . . .' His voice became rather more tense. 'And then will you please give him this letter?' He handed an envelope to Temple, who studied it thoughtfully.

'Mr John Richmond,' he repeated, as if he were trying to place the name. 'Why yes, I'll do that with pleasure.'

Lindsay gave him a searching look.

'Please realise that this is most important,' he said earnestly. 'Under no circumstances must you give the letter to anyone else – under no circumstances.'

'But supposing this Mr Richmond doesn't happen to be staying at the inn?' asked Temple.

'He'll be there all right,' declared Lindsay with quiet confidence.

'Why didn't you stop me when you first saw the car a quarter of a mile back?' Temple wanted to know.

'I was afraid that you might be—someone else.'

Temple glanced up sharply. There was an honest, straightforward look in the young man's eyes, so he pursued the question no further.

'Don't worry about the letter. I'll see that your friend gets it all right. It's a straight road into the village, I gather?'

'Perfectly. You can't possibly go wrong. The "Royal Gate" is on the left-hand side, about halfway through.'

'Thanks,' said Temple, lifting the latch.

'Ye're forgetting your postcards,' Mrs Moffat reminded him.

'So I am,' he smiled, picking up the envelope. 'Good night!'

When the door had closed, David Lindsay turned to Mrs Moffat, who had been an interested spectator.

'Mrs Moffat, I'm sorry to trouble you, but do you think I might use your 'phone?'

'I'm very sorry, Mr Lindsay,' she replied with great deliberation, 'but the telephone's out of order. It has been ever since yon storm started.'

This was obviously a blow to Lindsay.

'I see,' he murmured, wrinkling his forehead in some perplexity.

'Ye can try it if ye like, of course,' offered Mrs Moffat.

'It won't be any use, though. The wires must have broken somewhere.'

'Yes, yes, all right,' murmured Lindsay, whose thoughts were now obviously elsewhere.

'If there's anything I can do, Mr Lindsay—'

'No, no, I'm afraid you can't do anything. Thanks all the same.' He wished her good night and departed. She went to the window and watched him until he was almost out of sight. Then she bolted the door cautiously, crossed to the telephone and picked up the old type earpiece.

'Hello? I want Inverdale 74 . . . Hello, is that you?' Her voice was almost a whisper now. 'Yes—he's been here. Just left . . . No . . . no, I couldn't. He gave a letter to a man who was—' There was an interruption which obviously irritated her. 'For God's sake, listen to me,' she snapped impatiently. 'He gave the letter to a man who happened to be in the shop at the time . . . Yes—it was addressed to a Mr John Richmond at the "Royal Gate".'

Suddenly Mrs Moffat replaced the receiver and permitted herself the luxury of a grim chuckle.

4

'That young man seemed to be in rather a hurry,' commented Steve, when Temple returned to the car.

He recounted what had happened in the little shop as they started rather cautiously on their way towards the village.

'He saw the car about a quarter of a mile before we stopped,' said Temple, after they had been travelling for about ten minutes.

'Then why didn't he stop us?'

'Yes, that's what I wanted to know,' said Temple. 'Apparently he was afraid we might be someone else.'

There was the sound of a motor horn behind them, and Temple glanced through his driving mirror to see a large Buick Tourer approaching at a reckless speed. For the second time the horn sounded with a note of urgency.

'By Timothy, this fellow's in a hurry,' commented Temple, slowing down a little and drawing into the side.

'He wants you to stop, darling,' said Steve, who had been looking through the back window.

'Stop?' cried Temple in amazement.

'Yes, he's making signs.'

The Buick shot past them, took the middle of the road, and slowed down at once.

Two men emerged from the Buick and approached Temple's car, which had now pulled up. The elder of the two, a well-dressed, dapper little man, came up to Temple with a smile of apology.

'Really, sir, I must apologise for stopping you like this,' he began, a shade too extravagantly.

'If you want the road to Inverdale—' put in Steve quite pleasantly.

'Unfortunately, madam, we are not interested in the road to Inverdale.'

'I think perhaps we had better introduce ourselves, Laurence,' said the second man, a suntanned, fairly elderly individual, who seemed rather like a native of the district.

'Why yes, of course,' agreed his companion. 'My name is van Draper. Doctor Laurence van Draper. This gentleman is Major Lindsay, a very close friend of mine. In fact, he is the father of that very excitable young man you met in the village – about ten minutes ago.'

'I see,' nodded Temple, who made no attempt to reciprocate where the introductions were concerned.

'I believe I am correct in saying my son gave you a letter,' proceeded Major Lindsay, whose real name was Guest.

Temple looked up quickly.

'Yes, that's quite true,' he admitted.

'The letter was addressed to a certain Mr John Richmond,' continued the Major evenly.

'Well?'

'I should esteem it a favour,' said Major Lindsay impressively, 'if you would be good enough to give the letter to Doctor van Draper.'

Temple leaned back slightly and shrewdly surveyed the Major. There was silence for a few moments.

'I'm sorry, Major,' decided Temple at length, 'but your son gave me explicit instructions that the letter was to be delivered to no one except Mr Richmond.'

'I'm afraid your task will be very difficult, sir. You see, there is no such person as John Richmond.'

'No such person?' repeated Temple in some surprise.

Van Draper came forward.

'Perhaps you'd better let me explain, Major.' He placed an arm on the car window and addressed Temple. 'David Lindsay, the man who gave you the letter, is unfortunately the victim of a rather peculiar – what shall we say – mental condition?'

'You mean that he isn't quite . . .' began Steve, and van Draper nodded.

'Precisely. He isn't quite responsible for certain of his actions. There's no real harm in the boy; in fact his condition

is rapidly responding to treatment. But there are occasions – tonight was one of them I'm afraid – when he's a
little—er— unbalanced.'

'I understand perfectly,' said Temple in a non-committal
voice.

'My treatment of the case is purely of a psychological
nature,' continued van Draper, 'and for that reason I should
rather like to have the letter he gave you. On the other hand,
if you feel a little dubious about handing over—'

'No, of course not, Doctor,' replied Temple. 'There's no
question of doubting your word. But tell me, how did you
know about the letter?'

It seemed as if van Draper was about to embark upon a
long explanation, but the Major cut in quickly: 'Mrs Moffat
rang us up. She knows all about David's weakness, and
understands.'

'Oh yes—of course,' murmured Temple. 'Here is the letter.'

'Thanks,' said the Major, placing the envelope in his
pocket. 'I'll move my car out of the way so you can get by.
I seem to have taken up all the road.'

With a brief nod the two men departed and presently
their car drew into the side of the road. Temple and Steve
shot past them and for a time neither spoke. Then suddenly
Temple began to chuckle and Steve looked up in surprise.
She could not see that there was any cause for amusement.

'Paul, what's the matter?'

'Have you ever heard such a ridiculous story in all your
life?' grinned Temple.

'You mean—what the doctor said?'

'Doctor! He's no more a doctor than I am,' scoffed
the novelist. 'The fellow didn't look like a doctor and, by
Timothy, he certainly didn't talk like one.'

'If you didn't believe his story,' said Steve, obviously puzzled, 'why did you give him the letter?'

'I didn't, my dear,' laughed Temple, diving in his coat pocket. 'I gave him the postcards. Six delightful views of Inverdale. Two by moonlight!'

5

Like so many Scottish hotels, the 'Royal Gate' was classified as an inn. It was, in fact, the only comfortable hotel in this small village, which had lately become fashionable as a centre for salmon fishers, deerstalkers, mountaineers and artistic dilettantes.

In a noble but misguided endeavour to cater for all tastes, the proprietors had placed a stag's antlers over the mantelpiece in the entrance hall, a huge stuffed salmon in a glass case at the foot of the stairs, and several anaemic aquatints on any stretch of wall that appeared inviting.

There was, of course, a barometer suspended somewhat precariously just inside the front door. This had been badly damaged in transit and had lost a considerable quantity of its mercury, but oddly enough no one ever commented upon its inaccuracy, though every visitor most certainly tapped it fiercely first thing in the morning.

Paul Temple and his wife had very little difficulty in finding the inn. They were welcomed by the host and hostess, Mr and Mrs Weston, who informed them that the place was full, but undertook to 'manage something'.

Temple and Steve were surprised and pleased to hear their hosts' broad cockney dialect. Ernie Weston had been a night porter in a London hotel, where he had met his wife, who was employed there as a chambermaid. She had apparently come to London from Yorkshire to find better paid work, and between them they soon managed to save a few hundred pounds, which constituted the 'ingoing' to the 'Royal Gate'.

Buxom Mrs Weston, with the North Country roses still unfaded in her cheeks, had soon taken a fancy to Steve.

'I think you'll be very comfortable 'ere,' she was saying. 'It may not be as palatial as some of these railway hotels, but the view's champion, anyway.'

Steve looked round the fairly small bedroom which was sparsely furnished but very clean.

'This room will do very nicely, thanks,' she smiled. Mrs Weston smoothed imaginary creases out of her apron and nodded pleasantly.

Her husband entered, carrying two large suitcases. He was rather out of breath and dropped them thankfully. 'I'll bring up the other stuff later,' he announced. 'Where do I put this?'

'That's all right – leave it to me,' said Temple.

Ernie Weston seemed quite pleased to obey. He was an inch or two shorter than his wife, a few years older and rather wizened in appearance. While Mrs Weston bustled around, fetching towels and other requisites, Ernie stood in the doorway looking on. He made no effort to go.

'You seem to be fairly busy,' remarked Steve conversationally. 'Is it always like this?'

'Crikey, no!' exploded Ernie. 'This place was a proper white elephant up till a couple o' months ago. Ain't that right, Mother?'

'Well, things 'ave certainly bucked up, there's no doubt about that,' agreed Mrs Weston cheerfully.

'Bucked up! Blimey, I should think they 'ave. I've been run off me feet for weeks from early morning till last thing at night. 'Ave you come far, sir?'

'We left Edinburgh this morning, about ten.'

25

'Pretty good goin',' commented Ernie. 'I expect you're feelin' a bit peckish?'

'Yes, we are rather,' admitted Steve.

'Dinner'll be on at any minute now – seven-thirty. You'll hear the gong,' said Ernie, adding whimsically, 'the gong was Mother's idea.'

His wife glared at him, then turned to Steve. 'We started getting so many "posh" folk here, I thought we'd better live up to it,' she explained. 'Would you like a wash and brush up, ma'am?'

She took Steve to the bathroom, leaving Temple alone with Ernie.

'I'll pop down and get the other stuff up, sir,' volunteered the landlord.

'No, just a minute.'

Ernie perched himself easily on the edge of a small table. Temple suddenly shot a question.

'Do you and your wife run this place?'

'That's right, sir. Weston's the name. Bin 'ere six months now.'

'Do you like it?'

'Well, it's a bit quiet, sir, after London.'

'The hotel seems pretty full at the moment.'

'Not 'arf. Everybody seems to 'ave made their minds up to go on 'oliday just now. Between you and me, sir, you wouldn't be 'aving this room if me and the missus weren't pally.' He chuckled to himself as he helped Temple to lift a case onto a small bench at the foot of the bed.

The novelist flung a pair of pale blue pyjamas onto his pillow, and asked: 'Have you anyone staying here named Richmond—John Richmond?'

'Why yes, sir!' said Ernie, rather startled. 'Is 'e a pal o' yours?'

26

'No, but I'd like a word with him.'

'Well, I think 'e's out, sir. But 'e'll soon be back for dinner.'

'Good. I'll see him then.'

Temple was a little dubious as to whether he should offer to tip his host, but Ernie accepted the coin with alacrity.

'Thank you, sir – and if you fancy anythin' tasty-like for dinner, just tell the missis.' He winked and departed.

Temple went on with his unpacking, whistling quietly to himself. He had almost finished, and was just debating as to whether he should open his wife's case, when there was a knock at the door.

'Come in,' called Temple, thinking it was Ernie with the other luggage.

The door opened and a voice with a Teutonic accent rasped: 'I trust I do not intrude, Mr Temple?'

Temple turned swiftly.

'Why, Doctor Steiner! Come in!' He held out his hand to the German, who appeared just a little embarrassed.

'I saw your name in the register,' he said rather shyly, 'and could not resist this opportunity of renewing our—transatlantic friendship.'

'It's delightful to see you again,' Temple assured him. 'But I *am* surprised. What are you doing in Scotland?'

'I am on holiday,' replied Steiner. 'Trying to forget that I am a Doctor of Philosophy at the University of Philadelphia. But it is not easy, I am afraid. These Scottish people are very interesting to a philosopher. They are in many ways highly religious and, shall we say, narrow-minded. And yet they worship their national poet, Robert Burns. You have, no doubt, heard of Burns?'

Having heard of little else since arriving in Scotland, Temple smiled and nodded.

'And yet again,' pursued the professor, 'the Scottish race frown upon divorce. They look upon marriage as sacred, binding and eternal. Yet it is easier to many in Scotland than anywhere else in the British Isles. Perhaps you can explain these inconsistencies, Mr Temple. I should be most happy to listen and to take notes.'

But before Temple could make any attempt to reply, the door opened quickly and Steve rushed in.

'Paul, the most amazing thing—' She stopped suddenly at the sight of Doctor Steiner.

'I thought you'd be surprised,' laughed Temple. 'Dr Steiner has just arrived. He spotted our name in the register.'

'Perhaps I am wasting my time on philosophy,' smiled Steiner as he shook hands with Steve. 'I should be a detective—yes?' He looked from one to the other. 'But surely you tell me on the 'plane that shortly you leave for the South of France?'

'Paul changed his mind,' Steve informed him. 'He thought it would be too hot.'

'I like that, I must say!' protested Temple.

'I am glad to see a man change his mind,' declared Steiner, with a twinkle in his grey eyes. 'Well, I do not think you will find it too hot in Scotland. B-r-r! I have never felt it so cold, not even in Philadelphia.'

'How long are you staying here, Doctor?' asked Temple.

'I don't know. It all depends—on the weather,' he added hurriedly. Rather unexpectedly Steiner turned towards the door. 'I must start unpacking. We shall meet later, I hope—at dinner.'

'Why, yes, of course. You must sit at our table. I'll arrange it,' said Temple.

'I shall be honoured. Then for the time being . . . *auf wiedersehen*!' He bowed slightly and went out. As the door closed Temple turned to his wife.

28

'Now, what's all this excitement about?' he demanded. 'You came dashing in here as if all the Campbells and McLeods were after you.'

'Paul, whom do you think I've seen?'

'I haven't the vaguest idea.'

'Iris!'

'Iris—here?' Temple ejaculated.

Steve nodded. She sat on the bed and tucked her legs under the eiderdown. 'Darling, I'm not joking,' she assured him seriously. 'I really have seen Iris – there's no mistaking her. I was coming out of the bathroom when a door opened at the far end of the corridor – and out stepped Iris.'

'Did she see you?' broke in Temple swiftly.

Steve wrinkled her forehead in some perplexity.

'I don't know,' she had to admit. 'I have a feeling that she did.'

'But—but what happened?' Temple was completely mystified.

'There's a staircase at the end of the corridor, near her room. Before I could say anything she had turned her back to me and disappeared.'

'Why didn't you call to her?'

'I was so startled – it was like one of those dreams when you feel quite helpless.'

'It's certainly very peculiar,' reflected Temple. 'What the devil would Iris be doing here?'

Suddenly, in the distance, a gong boomed.

'Dinner! And I haven't even started to unpack!' cried Steve. Temple appeared not to have heard. He was sitting on the edge of a chair gazing thoughtfully out of the window – though he actually saw nothing of the view so highly praised by his hostess. Steve may have made a mistake about Iris, but it was hardly likely. What could she be doing in a remote Scottish inn! Why had she thrown over the best part of her career to penetrate the wilds of Scotland? Why . . .

He was startled by Steve's hand on his shoulder. 'Paul, I've just remembered about that letter. Hadn't you better inquire—?'

He smiled at her. 'I have.'

'Then there is a John Richmond?'

'Certainly.'

Steve considered this.

'Paul, you don't think there could be any connection between the young man, those two men who stopped us, and Iris?'

Temple frowned. Once again the gong boomed and almost simultaneously there was a knock on the door. When Temple opened it, Ernie Weston stood outside.

'I beg your pardon, sir, but I believe you wanted to see Mr Richmond. I brought him up now because I thought you might—'

'Oh yes, please ask him to come in.'

The man who had been waiting just along the corridor came forward.

'Why, Sir—' began Temple. Then stopped at an urgent sign from the visitor.

'Sir Graham!' cried Steve, before they could suppress her exclamation.

'There seems to be some mistake,' said Sir Graham Forbes politely. 'My name is Richmond. John Richmond.'

CHAPTER II

Concerning Z.4

1

Temple was the first to appreciate that there was a serious element to the situation. He recognised an urgent note in Sir Graham's voice. Obviously, the Chief Commissioner was not anxious to have his identity revealed. As there was every indication of Steve starting an inquiry of this nature, Temple suddenly broke into a rather nonsensical chuckle.

'Really, sir, we must beg your forgiveness,' he grinned. 'By Timothy, I've never seen anything like it. . .' He regarded Sir Graham quizzically, his head on one side. 'The same chin, the same nose . . . Why, he's just like old Forbes, isn't he, Steve? The absolute "spit" of old Forbes – just look at his hair . . . well, I'm damned!'

He contrived to shoot a warning glance at Steve while Ernie Weston was looking at Sir Graham.

'What the devil is all this about?' snapped Forbes irritably, addressing the landlord. 'Who are this lady and gentleman?'

Ernie Weston was palpably perplexed.

'A Mr and Mrs Temple, sir,' he informed Sir Graham. 'Arrived about half an hour ago.' He looked at each of them in turn. 'There seems to have been some sort of mistake, doesn't there?' he suggested.

'I thought you said they wanted to see me,' growled Forbes.

'Well, 'e said 'e did want to see you,' protested Ernie. He turned on Temple rather fiercely. 'I say, what's the game?' he almost snarled. 'You said I was to give a message to . . .'

'It's all right,' laughed Temple. 'There's nothing to get excited about. This gentleman reminded us of someone else, that's all.'

Ernie made no effort to move. 'But this is the gent you wanted to see – Mr Richmond—' he began in puzzled tones.

By this time, Steve had begun to realise the position.

He broke off suddenly, as if realising Weston's presence for the first time. 'It's all right, Weston,' he murmured casually. But Ernie was obviously loath to accept this dismissal.

'We don't serve dinner after a quarter to,' he announced.

'We shall bear that in mind,' replied Temple, politely holding the door for him.

'All right,' said the landlord, retreating reluctantly.

Temple watched him down the corridor, then carefully closed the door. Steve sank on the bed with a sigh of relief, while Sir Graham perched on the arm of a chair.

'Sir Graham, I'm most terribly sorry,' Temple apologised. 'It was extremely stupid of us both to blurt out like that.'

'That's all right,' said Forbes gruffly. 'You covered it up well.' He ruminated rather gloomily for a few seconds, then suddenly asked: 'What the devil are you two doing here?'

Temple and Steve exchanged a brief smile.

'Well, if it comes to that—' began the novelist.

'I know, I know!' Forbes forestalled him. 'Don't ask me, Temple. Don't ask me!' He drew a hand across his forehead rather wearily, then continued: 'But seriously, what made you two visit Inverdale? You couldn't have had an inkling . . . it isn't possible . . .'

'You remember we told you we were coming to Scotland,' Steve reminded him.

'So you did. Yes, I'd forgotten about that,' Sir Graham admitted. But there was a dubious note in his voice.

'Sir Graham, don't you think you might tell us why you are staying here under the name of Richmond?' suggested Temple mildly.

'Yes, that's another thing, Temple. You asked to see Mr John Richmond. I *am* John Richmond, though how the devil—'

'Paul, give him the letter,' interrupted Steve. 'Then we can go down to dinner.' There was a note of urgency in her voice.

'What letter?' demanded Forbes quickly, looking from one to the other.

'A letter from a young man named Lindsay—David Lindsay,' explained Temple.

'For me?' queried Forbes in some surprise.

Temple nodded.

'I don't know anyone named David Lindsay. There must be some mistake.'

Steve was quite taken aback. 'You don't know anyone called Lindsay?' she repeated in amazement.

'No,' said Forbes decisively.

'Is there another John Richmond staying here?'

'Not to my knowledge.'

'Then this letter *must* be for you,' declared Steve.

Temple, who had been pacing the room, his hands deep in his trouser pockets, looked up and smiled.

'This gets brighter and brighter!' he said. 'First of all I meet the delightful Mrs Moffat, then the excitable Mr Lindsay, and later—'

'Mrs Moffat?' interrupted Forbes. 'You mean the woman in the village?'

'That's right,' nodded Temple. 'The dark-eyed beauty with a sister in Peckham.' Sir Graham pondered upon this for a moment, then asked: 'How did you meet Mrs Moffat?'

Temple was gazing thoughtfully out of the window at the view so highly praised by his hostess, so Steve began to explain.

'On our way here, Sir Graham, we got lost. We stopped in the village, and to make absolutely certain of getting on the right road—'

'I popped into Mrs Moffat's,' put in Temple suddenly becoming aware of the conversation once more. 'Just as I was on the verge of leaving, in barged the young fellow I was telling you about – David Lindsay. He was obviously excited and rather worried about something. To cut a long story short, he asked me if I was coming into Inverdale, and whether I'd deliver a letter for him to a Mr John Richmond, who happened to be staying at the "Royal Gate". Naturally, I agreed to do so. On the way here, however, two men stopped us—'

Sir Graham looked up sharply. 'Can you describe them?'

'There was a man who called himself Doctor Laurence van Draper, and another, rather military-looking chap, who said that he was Major Lindsay, father of the young man who gave me the letter. They told us a rather one-sided story about the young fellow being a bit mental, and more or less demanded the letter. They were quite nice about it, but obviously meant business.'

'What happened?' demanded Forbes eagerly.

'Well, Paul happened to buy a packet of postcards, which Mrs Moffat fortunately popped into an envelope,' smiled Steve.

'You don't mean you gave them the postcards?' asked Forbes, jumping up.

'I'm afraid so,' Temple replied evenly.

'Well, I'm damned!' Forbes sank back and slapped his thigh in approval. Temple wandered off to the window again.

'Now listen, Temple. This is most important. I want you to describe that young man as closely as possible.'

Temple swung round.

'You mean Lindsay? Oh, he was about five feet ten – dark – good-looking—'

'Rather like Frank Lawton, the film actor,' supplied Steve.

'My God, it's Hammond all right!' ejaculated Forbes, thumping his fist on the table. 'Now, of course, I understand.'

Temple had crossed to a chair and picked up the jacket he had been wearing earlier in the day. As he dived into an inside pocket, a look of concern spread over his features.

'Darling, what is it?' asked Steve.

'The letter . . .' gasped Temple.

Forbes went across to him quickly. 'Temple, you don't mean to say—'

'It's gone,' announced Temple quietly.

'Gone!' echoed Steve. 'But, Paul, it couldn't possibly—'

'You didn't make a mistake about those postcards, Temple?' suggested Sir Graham.

'No. I had the letter when I arrived here. I'm absolutely certain of that. When I was unpacking, I changed into this old sports coat and left the other on the chair.'

'That letter's important, Temple,' said Sir Graham in some anxiety. 'It's desperately important, and we've got to get it back.'

Temple's brain was working quickly.

'Those men – van Draper and the fellow who called himself Major Lindsay – they must have contacted someone here at the "Royal Gate". . .'

Forbes nodded thoughtfully.

'Who did you see when you arrived?' he asked.

'A porter helped us with the luggage, then Weston and his wife brought us upstairs.'

Temple carefully examined the contents of every pocket without result.

'Paul, there's Doctor Steiner,' Steve suddenly reminded him. 'He came in here after Weston and—'

'By Timothy, yes! And he stood over by that chair for quite a while. But how could he possibly know—'

'Steiner?' put in Forbes. 'Who exactly is Doctor Steiner?'

'He's a Professor of Philosophy at Philadelphia University,' said Temple. 'We met him on the *Golden Clipper*, coming over here.'

'What's he doing in Scotland?'

'He's on holiday. As soon as he spotted our names in the register he came up here.' Temple paused and puckered his brow.

'By Timothy! I'm a prize jackass if you like!' he ejaculated.

'What do you mean?' asked Steve.

'Steve, don't you remember? I didn't sign a register. The book was full. Weston made me sign on a sheet of notepaper. He put the paper in a drawer, so I don't see how Steiner could possibly have—'

'Then he knew you were coming here,' cried Forbes. 'He was waiting for you – waiting for the letter!'

'Just a minute. Not so fast, Sir Graham,' softly interposed Temple.

'Why should Doctor Steiner, a respectable university professor, want that letter?' asked Steve.

'I presume you have only his word for his identity,' said Forbes. 'What's his nationality?'

'Oh, obviously Austrian, I should say. Most probably Viennese,' said Temple.

'Well, it seems a remarkable coincidence that he should be staying here the very night that Noel Hammond—'

'Who is Noel Hammond?' demanded Temple. 'And who's this man Draper? And who the devil is—'

'I can't tell you now, Temple,' snapped Forbes. 'Come to my room after dinner—no, I'll come down here. It will be safer. We must get that letter back – no matter what happens we must get that letter!'

He regarded them both with a grim smile. 'I think you will be interested to know why I came to Scotland instead of going to the South of France.'

He turned to the door. 'I'll see you both here, in about an hour.'

'Yes, all right,' agreed Temple.

After Forbes had departed, Temple carefully folded his coat and placed it in a drawer. Neither spoke for a minute or two, then Steve suggested they should go down to dinner. Her husband was busy unlocking a suitcase, and did not appear to be listening.

'Is anything the matter, Steve?' he said suddenly.

'No – nothing,' she replied with a tiny gulp, but he could see that her eyes were slightly misty.

'You're worried, aren't you?' he challenged her, taking hold of her shoulders and looking at her closely. 'You're upset about this business.'

'Yes,' admitted Steve at length.

'Why?'

She sighed.

'Well, so many things have started like this, haven't they? The Front Page Men, that awful business with the Knave of Diamonds, and—'

Temple gave her shoulder a gentle squeeze. 'Darling, if you want to leave here first thing in the morning – we leave. And nothing on earth will stop us.'

'You're very sweet,' whispered Steve gently, rubbing her cheek against his rough tweed coat. Somewhere below a gong boomed insistently. Temple smiled.

'I rather fancy that's for our benefit,' he said.

2

An hour later two men knocked cautiously at the door of Mrs Moffat's shop. They seemed reluctant to be seen, but they need not have feared, for practically every person in that tiny hamlet was in bed, though it was little after nine. There was a sound of bolts being withdrawn, and Mrs Moffat eventually peered through the few inches between door and lintel. When she recognised them she opened the door swiftly, and they went inside.

'What happened?' she demanded quickly, setting the flickering candle on the counter and facing them.

'We missed him,' growled van Draper.

Mrs Moffat eyed them suspiciously.

'It's no good hiding things, Draper,' said Guest. 'She'll have to know sooner or later.'

'Something went wrong?' speculated Mrs Moffat, leaning an elbow on the counter.

Guest nodded. 'We stopped the car and dished out a cock and bull story about Lindsay being out of his mind. They seemed to swallow it all right, but . . .'

He took the packet of postcards from his pocket.

'Instead of handing over the letter, he presented us with these damn things!'

Mrs Moffat recognised the envelope with a grim smile. Taking out the postcards, she carefully replaced them on the stand.

'That was canny of ye both, I must say,' was her only comment.

'We can't stand here all night,' snorted van Draper impatiently. 'Let's go upstairs.'

But Mrs Moffat did not offer to move.

'Why are ye both so anxious to get that letter?' she persisted. 'What was in it?'

'I've had my suspicions about Lindsay for a long time,' said van Draper. 'Tonight they were—'

'My God!' cried Mrs Moffat suddenly, her face grotesquely distorted by the guttering candlelight. 'Ye don't mean to say he's—'

'His name is Hammond – Noel Hammond,' replied van Draper with savage deliberation. 'He's a British Agent. We ought to have checked up on him long ago, instead of accepting one person's word.'

'But Z.2 recommended him,' insisted Mrs Moffat. 'She swore he was safe.'

'The little fool was taken in by him,' said Guest contemptuously.

'Z.2. That's Iris Archer, isn't it?' queried van Draper thoughtfully. 'She's always liable to fall for that type. That's her one weakness. We should have realised that.'

Mrs Moffat set her lips in a firm line of disapproval. 'You have always said that Lindsay was a good man at his job,' she reminded them.

'Hardwick always said so,' van Draper agreed. 'Though just lately they don't seem to have been hitting it off too well.'

'Well, whatever happens, we've got to get Lindsay,' declared Guest in ruthless tones.

'That's imperative,' said van Draper.

'Why is it so imperative?' Mrs Moffat wanted to know.

'Why?' spluttered van Draper impatiently. 'Good God, woman, don't you realise that Lindsay can blow up the whole bag of tricks? He's been working with Hardwick on the screen . . . he knows about us – about Z.4—'

'About Z.4?' put in Mrs Moffat rapidly. 'What exactly does he know about Z.4?'

'He knows that Z.4 is behind Hardwick,' said van Draper slowly. 'Also that Z.4 is at the head of the greatest espionage organisation in Europe.'

'But does he know who Z.4 is?' pursued Mrs Moffat.

Guest shrugged his shoulders. 'Do any of us?'

'That's not the point,' van Draper cut in. 'Lindsay or Hammond, whichever you like to call him, knows a great deal too much. There's Hardwick to start with . . .'

'And don't you think the British Intelligence people know about Hardwick?' suggested Mrs Moffat.

'Of course they do,' retorted van Draper. 'But fortunately for us they don't attach any importance to him – yet.'

'And after receiving Hammond's letter they might?'

'Precisely.'

'I wonder who this man . . . Richmond is?' speculated Guest.

'I don't know – but if he's got that letter we've got to get him before he leaves.'

'I shouldn't be surprised if Lindsay hasn't seen Richmond himself,' theorised Mrs Moffat.

'No,' interrupted van Draper. 'Lindsay would keep clear of the village. I'm sure of that. He'd reckon on us keeping an eye on the "Royal Gate" – that's why he didn't ask our friend for a lift.'

'You know, I've got a hunch that Lindsay might return,' said Guest thoughtfully.

'You mean—here?' queried Mrs Moffat, rather taken aback.

'Yes, here.'

'Why should he?'

'Well, in the first place,' Guest elaborated, 'he doesn't suspect that you happen to be one of us, and he'll probably be anxious to try and contact Richmond by telephone.'

The words were hardly out of his mouth when the telephone rang.

'I have it switched through upstairs,' explained Mrs Moffat succinctly. 'We'd all better go up.'

She picked up the candle and led the way towards the crude staircase, and they gingerly climbed up to the top landing. The telephone rang again, louder now, and Mrs Moffat opened the door of a small room which was built in the roof of the cottage. Roughly furnished with a divan, a table and two or three chairs, it was lighted by a small dormer window in the daytime.

Mrs Moffat picked up the telephone, which stood on the floor at the side of the divan.

'Hello? . . . Yes . . . When did you arrive? . . . When? . . . I see.' She covered the mouthpiece for a moment and whispered to the two men: 'It's Z.2.'

'Yes, I'm listening,' she spoke into the instrument again. 'Who?' Her face became noticeably alert, even in that dim light. '. . . Paul Temple?' she repeated somewhat incredulously. 'What's he like? . . . Yes, describe him quickly . . . yes—'

'Ask her to come down here,' broke in van Draper urgently. 'She might know something about Richmond.'

Mrs Moffat nodded.

'We want to see you . . . yes, straight away. Get here as soon as you can.' She replaced the receiver.

'So that was Z.2,' murmured Guest thoughtfully. 'I rather thought she was out of things.'

'We needed her on this job. Z.4 ordered her up here,' said van Draper.

Mrs Moffat was busy lighting a rather smoky oil lamp. When she had it working to her satisfaction she turned and asked them: 'Do ye know who the gentleman was who handed ye the postcards?'

'Not the faintest idea,' snapped van Draper. He thought he saw a gleam of amusement in her cold eyes. 'Who was it?' he demanded suspiciously.

'Paul Temple,' replied Mrs Moffat simply.

'Phew! Paul Temple!' whistled Guest. 'My God, if Temple's on this job we can expect fireworks.'

'What the devil is Paul Temple doing here?' demanded van Draper fiercely.

Mrs Moffat gave the merest lift of the shoulders, but did not reply. Instead, she busied herself with the lamp once more.

'You don't suppose Temple happens to be Richmond, by any chance?' suggested Guest. 'That would account for his switching the postcards.'

'Lindsay would have recognised him,' said Mrs Moffat, without turning.

'Not necessarily,' persisted the other. 'After all, none of us know who Z.4 is, but we take orders from him – or her.'

'We should hear something about Richmond from Z.2,' decided van Draper after a moody silence. 'If she's staying at the "Royal Gate", then obviously she must have seen Richmond.'

'Sh!' called Mrs Moffat suddenly. Her keen ears had detected the lifting of the front door latch, and this was suddenly confirmed by the ringing of the shop bell.

'Who can it be at this time?' asked van Draper.

'I shan't be long,' said Mrs Moffat, making for the door.

'Wait!' ordered van Draper.

She paused. 'Well?'

'It might be Lindsay. If he wants to use the telephone – it's in order now. You understand?'

She nodded. They heard her descend in leisurely fashion, and presently voices floated up from below.

'It's Hammond!' whispered Guest, and his confederate nodded.

'Somehow or other, I thought he'd turn up,' murmured van Draper. 'Right from the beginning I had a feeling we'd get him. Is your gun here?'

Guest nodded. 'If only Temple hadn't tricked us over that letter, we'd be sitting pretty now we've got Hammond,' said Guest.

Van Draper motioned him to be silent as footsteps were heard on the stairs.

'You never told me you had the 'phone connected up here,' Lindsay was saying as the door swung open.

'Hello, Lindsay! Surprised?' said van Draper.

'Why, hello, Van, I didn't expect—'

'Drop that gun!' called Guest sharply. A tiny revolver fell from Lindsay's left hand onto the wooden floor.

There was silence for some seconds.

43

'What's the idea?' asked Lindsay at length.

'There seems to have been a slight misunderstanding,' smiled Guest. 'Don't you agree, Mr Lindsay – or should I say Hammond?'

Lindsay was obviously exerting every ounce of self-control.

'Hammond? Who the devil is Hammond?' he demanded.

'Your name is Hammond, my friend,' van Draper informed him with cruel deliberation; 'Noel Hammond, of the British Intelligence Department.' His tone was scathing now, but Lindsay broke into a laugh which sounded surprisingly genuine.

'British Intelligence?' he repeated. 'That's damned funny. If I'm from the British Intelligence, why the devil do you think I worked with Hardwick? I've sweated my guts out on that blasted screen of his.'

'Oh yes,' agreed van Draper. 'You worked very hard on the screen – we'll grant you that. But you had a reason,' he added viciously.

'Of course I had a reason,' replied Lindsay. 'Six thousand reasons, to be exact.'

'Six thousand?' echoed Mrs Moffat. 'Did Z.4 promise you six thousand pounds if—'

'No – dollars,' replied Lindsay cynically. 'I say, what the devil is all this about, anyway?' He looked round desperately. The two revolvers never wavered. Mrs Moffat's ample form continued to fill the doorway.

'Two years ago,' van Draper was saying, 'a certain Mr John Hardwick approached the War Office concerning an invention of his called the Hardwick Screen. This was tested and proved, to all intents and purposes, to be a failure—'

'And then I suppose the British Intelligence Department sent me along just in case?' suggested Lindsay sarcastically.

'Yes,' agreed van Draper quietly, 'just in case a certain other party became interested in the screen and any future developments.'

'I've never heard such damned nonsense in my life,' cried Lindsay indignantly. 'If the War Office thought the screen was a washout, why should the Intelligence Department take an interest in the affair?'

'The answer to that is quite simple, my friend,' put in Guest smoothly. 'They're after Z.4.'

'Very interesting, I'm sure,' said Lindsay, trying hard to appear cynical.

'The Intelligence Department discovered that Z.4 had contacted Hardwick,' pursued van Draper evenly, 'so they determined to kill two birds with one stone. Keep away from that door!' he commanded suddenly, as he noticed Lindsay's glance move in that direction.

'Now listen to me, van Draper,' began Lindsay nervously. 'Put that revolver away and don't be a fool. Surely we can talk this over sensibly.'

'What was in that letter you sent to Richmond?' demanded van Draper inexorably.

'And who is John Richmond?' said Guest.

'I—I haven't the slightest idea what you are talking about,' stammered Lindsay, who was obviously rattled.

'That's a pity,' sneered van Draper, 'because I'm going to give you fifteen seconds to refresh your memory.'

He took a watch from his pocket. 'Keep him covered, Guest,' he ordered.

Lindsay looked round once more in desperation.

'Five,' said van Draper imperturbably.

Lindsay moistened his lips, then looked at Mrs Moffat. She returned his stare with eyes that were quite expressionless. There could be no help from that quarter.

'Ten!' snapped van Draper.

'You—you can't do this!' shrieked Lindsay hysterically. He made a sudden dive for the door. Both revolvers barked, and Lindsay fell with a choking gasp across the small table. Mrs Moffat saved the lamp just in time. She picked up the table and replaced the lamp on it as if nothing had happened.

'Pity he didn't talk,' commented van Draper unemotionally.

Suddenly the shop bell tinkled.

3

Guest looked somewhat alarmed. 'Could anyone have heard?' he whispered.

'It's probably Z.2,' Mrs Moffat told him in a scornful voice, as she prepared to go down.

'If it is Archer, get her up here,' ordered Guest through the half-open door.

Meanwhile, van Draper had been briskly searching the dead man's pockets, but had found nothing to enlighten him. He eyed the body distastefully. 'We'll have to get this out of the way. . . Better get the car and heave him over Moorford Ridge,' he decided. Before they could make any further plans, Iris Archer entered the room. She wore a smart tweed suit, carried a Robin Hood hat, and appeared, as usual, completely self-possessed.

'Hello, Laurence,' she greeted van Draper. 'How long have you been up here?' Then she saw the body of David Lindsay, with the ominous red stain trickling down the sloping floorboards. Iris caught her breath.

'David!'

She made a movement towards the body.

'Don't touch him!' cried Guest sharply.

Iris looked at them in complete bewilderment.

46

'I'm sorry – and particularly sorry because he was a— friend of yours,' said van Draper grimly, 'but we have had to dispose of Mr David Lindsay.'

'But—why?' cried Iris, with a shudder.

'His name was Hammond,' explained Guest drily. 'He was working for the Intelligence people.'

Iris was patently staggered, and leaned on the table for support. There was a frightened look in her eyes now.

'My God, I hope you don't think that I—' she was beginning.

'No,' said Guest. 'He had his tracks well covered.'

'Why, it's . . . it's unbelievable,' breathed Iris incoherently. 'I ran into Lindsay two years ago . . . he had a police record from here to Tokyo. I checked up on him before I even mentioned him to Z.4.' Neither of the men had ever seen her appear as alarmed as this. 'Honestly, Laurence,' she whispered, 'I never even suspected—'

'That's all right,' van Draper reassured her. 'Hammond was a clever devil. He even convinced us that he was on the level.'

After a while she calmed down and seated herself in one of the uncomfortable chairs.

'When did you arrive?' asked Guest.

'Last night. How are things going?'

'Perfectly.'

'Is the screen ready?'

'Almost. We are waiting for Z.4.'

This startled Iris. 'You mean you are waiting for instructions from Z.4?' she corrected him.

'No,' said Mrs Moffat, speaking for the first time.

'We mean we are waiting for Z.4,' insisted van Draper quietly.

'Don't be ridiculous,' laughed Iris. 'He's kept us in the dark so far, why should he—'

'This time Z.4 is coming out into the open,' reiterated van Draper. 'He's got to.'

'When?'

'Very soon, we hope,' replied Mrs Moffat.

'How do you know this?' asked Iris quickly.

'Mrs Moffat had a letter almost two weeks ago,' said Guest. 'He's got four syndicates interested in the screen, and they are all willing to pay over five million. The price may rise even higher – stimulated by competition. A million is neither here nor there to a government in this crazy armaments race.'

'And how shall we know Z.4 when he arrives?' Iris was anxious to discover.

'I shall know him,' slowly announced Mrs Moffat, 'by a quotation.'

She closed her lips firmly, and did not seem inclined for any further confidences. Iris rather shakily powdered her nose, and the men lit cigarettes.

'Iris,' said Guest after a while, 'there's a man staying at the inn called Richmond. John Richmond. Have you seen him?'

'Why, no. Who is he?'

'We have reason to suspect he's a British Agent. Lindsay sent him a letter, and we've got to know what was in it.'

The stress on the last sentence was unmistakable, and Iris nodded thoughtfully.

She changed her mind about smoking, and took a small cigarette from a dainty shagreen case.

'A British Agent,' she ruminated.

'What are you thinking of?' asked van Draper.

'I was just wondering if Paul Temple happened to be John Richmond.'

'That's what I thought,' agreed Guest eagerly.

Van Draper frowned thoughtfully for some moments. Then he appeared to come to a decision. Abruptly he stubbed out his cigarette and addressed Iris.

'Get hold of Temple tonight,' he ordered. 'If necessary, go through his room.'

'It might be a good idea to get Temple out of the way,' Guest murmured tentatively. 'Even if he doesn't happen to be Richmond, he's probably even more dangerous. I can't think he is merely up here for the good of his health.'

'Yes,' agreed van Draper after some thought. 'Yes, I think you're right.'

'You mean . . . tonight?' demanded Iris in a surprised tone.

'Tonight,' insisted van Draper, quietly but firmly. 'As to the exact method, I leave that to you. Probably the situation will suggest something.'

He lit another cigarette, and the three of them smoked for some seconds without speaking.

'Mrs Moffat,' called Iris at length, and the dour woman came forward. Iris regarded her curiously, wondering why Z.4 should choose to take her into his confidence.

'Mrs Moffat, you said that you would recognise Z.4 by a quotation,' she began.

'I did,' said Mrs Moffat decisively.

'And the quotation?' persisted Iris.

Mrs Moffat smiled.

'What was it Shakespeare said – about travellers?'

4

Paul Temple and Steve had no complaints to make about dinner. The salmon trout in particular had been excellent and Paul Temple had even gone so far as to compliment his hostess upon it. The coffee had also been to their taste – creamy and not too strong, quite unlike the muddy mixture that goes by this name in most provincial hotels. And now Temple had been persuaded to smoke one of Sir Graham's favourite cigars, which was not proving so overpowering as he had anticipated.

The novelist had just completely surprised Forbes by announcing that he and his wife proposed to continue their journey the next morning.

'Steve has already been through quite enough for me in the past,' argued Temple.

'I can quite see your point of view,' nodded Sir Graham, 'but I don't think you realise the seriousness of the situation.'

'I promised Steve we should leave here first thing in the morning,' declared Temple firmly, 'and I intend to keep my promise, Sir Graham.'

There was a pause. Then Sir Graham leaned forward and spoke distinctly.

'I'm sorry, Temple, but I'm afraid it's out of the question.'

'What do you mean?' cried Steve in some alarm.

Forbes settled himself in his chair again.

'Perhaps it might simplify matters if I told you something about this business,' he suggested. 'I can't tell you everything, Temple, for obvious reasons, but . . . well, I suppose I'd better start at the beginning, although where the devil the beginning is exactly, it's difficult to say.' He puffed hard at his cigar for some moments. 'About two years ago a man named John Hardwick got in touch with the War Office concerning an invention of his which he called the Hardwick Screen. Hardwick himself was a chemist who had inherited a large sum of money from some aunt or other.'

'What was this invention, exactly?' asked Temple.

'The Hardwick Screen was a system of camouflage for use on land, its chief advantage being—'

'You mean a smoke screen, similar to the sort of thing used at sea?'

'Well, in a way, yes. But Hardwick's Screen differed from the kind of thing used by the Admiralty in several rather important details. However, that doesn't concern us at the moment.'

'Had Hardwick invented a lamp or beam of some sort that could penetrate the screen?' asked Temple.

Forbes nodded eagerly.

'He had, Temple. And that is more or less where our story starts. The War Office gave the screen a try-out, and, to be brief, it was a terrible flop. The screen itself was all right, but the beam was a dismal failure. Without the beam, of course, the whole bag of tricks was a washout. Hardwick had the devil of a row with the War Office, and came back to Scotland.'

He paused to relight his cigar, which had gone out.

'After Hardwick had returned to Scotland,' he continued at length, 'the Intelligence people began taking an interest in the matter.'

'You mean the Secret Service?' queried Steve, who had had some experience of that department in her reporting days.

'If you prefer the term, Steve. Yes, the Secret Service.'

'But why should the Intelligence people be interested in the screen if the War Office had already turned it down?'

'I'm glad you asked that question, Temple,' said Sir Graham weightily, 'because it's the crux of the whole matter. Do you mind if I have another cup of coffee, Steve?'

Steve poured out the coffee.

'Go on, Sir Graham,' urged Temple.

'For many years now,' continued Sir Graham, 'the British Intelligence Department, and Scotland Yard, too, for that matter, have realised that there existed in Europe one of the greatest independent espionage organisations of all time. An organisation under the direct control of one man – or woman.' He paused then added dramatically: 'Someone under the pseudonym of Z.4.'

'Z.4?' said Temple softly.

'But what country do these people represent?' It was Steve who asked the question.

'They represent no country – and any country,' replied Sir Graham somewhat enigmatically.

'You mean these people trade in official secrets, irrespective of their origin?' queried Temple.

'Exactly. Now, after Hardwick had returned to Scotland, the British Intelligence had a hunch that Z.4 or one of his organisation would contact Hardwick.'

'I can't see why,' said Temple, wrinkling his forehead. 'If the Hardwick screen had already proved a failure, why should it interest Z.4?'

'I've got it!' cried Steve suddenly. 'You circulated a report that the test had been successful, knowing that under those circumstances Z.4 was almost bound to contact Hardwick.'

'Roughly, that was the idea,' conceded Sir Graham.

'And a damned good idea, too,' approved Temple.

'But we didn't let it rest there,' continued the Chief Commissioner. 'A young fellow named Hammond, a brilliant research chemist and also a member of the British Intelligence, had been interested in the Hardwick Screen from the very first. He was also interested – like everyone else in the Secret Service – in the identity of Z.4. Being a clever young devil, Hammond, or David Lindsay as he called himself, discovered that Iris Archer, your friend the actress, was a member of Z.4's organisation.'

Steve looked at the Chief Commissioner in complete amazement.

'He played up to her like blazes,' pursued Sir Graham, 'and before very long he found himself working side by side with her, and also directly in touch with Hardwick.'

During his last few words there had appeared to be a faint tap at the door. As he paused, it was repeated, gently but clearly.

Temple motioned to Steve to remain where she was, went silently across the room and swiftly opened the door.

There was no one to be seen.

Temple turned in some perplexity.

'There's a note on the floor,' Forbes pointed out, and Temple stooped to pick it up.

'My God!' he ejaculated, turning the letter over and examining it. 'It's the letter that Lindsay gave me. I recognise the envelope.'

'Doesn't seem to have been opened either,' said Forbes excitedly, almost snatching it out of Temple's hand, and tearing open the envelope.

'It seems strange that it should be returned like this – unopened,' mused Steve, while Sir Graham was rapidly scanning the contents.

'Listen to this!' he exclaimed.

'*Identity of Z.4 unknown, even by important members of the organisation. Believe Z.4 to be in Scotland and likely to contact headquarters within the next three weeks. Have been compelled to work with Hardwick on behalf of Z.4. John Hardwick now prisoner at Skerry Lodge.*'

'Looks like double-crossing,' commented Temple.

'My God, Temple! Listen to this,' continued Sir Graham.

'*Screen of definite value and importance. Beam almost perfected. Imperative Hardwick rescued. Contact Major Foster at once – N.H.*'

'Screen of definite value – beam almost perfected,' repeated Temple with unconscious dramatic effect.

'I must get to a telephone,' decided Forbes at once, but before he could move there was a knock at the door, which was gingerly opened. Mrs Weston stood there.

'Mrs Temple is wanted on the 'phone – from London,' she announced.

'Wanted on the telephone?' repeated Steve, completely surprised.

'That's right,' nodded Mrs Weston. 'They didn't say who it was.'

'But no one knows you're here, Steve,' Temple pointed out.

'No—no, of course not,' she agreed.

'That's damned funny, if you like,' muttered Sir Graham. 'I'll come with you, Steve, then maybe I can get my call when you've finished.'

'Yes, all right,' agreed Steve. 'Shan't be a minute, darling.'

After they had gone, Temple paced steadily up and down the room, digesting the events of the past few hours. Originally, he had looked forward to these few days as an opportunity to work out in full detail the plot of his latest novel. Now he dismissed the idea of even starting to concentrate upon it. The idea of this espionage organisation was completely new, and greatly intrigued him. That Iris Archer should be a member was even more intriguing. But there had always been an element of mystery about Iris, reflected Temple. She disappeared from the stage far too often; and not even the gossip writers were able to discover her whereabouts.

With his back to the door, Temple was suddenly conscious that it had opened softly. He swung round.

Iris Archer stood in the doorway, looking more beautiful than he had ever seen her.

'Why, Iris!' cried Temple, injecting as much astonishment into his voice as possible.

'Surprised?' she demanded softly.

'Well, it does seem a long way from the South of France,' he said flippantly.

'Are you going to ask me to sit down, or do I have to explain standing up?' she smiled.

Temple hastened to offer her a chair.

'Where's Steve?'

'She's downstairs telephoning. She won't be long,' replied Temple. He surveyed her shrewdly. There was something behind this visit. Did she want the letter, or—

'What made you come to Scotland, Iris?' he asked.

'Darling, I didn't know what to do. My doctor said I should go to Cornwall, I fancied the Riviera, so naturally—'

'You struck a happy medium and came to Scotland.'

'Exactly,' laughed Iris, casually producing her shagreen cigarette case. 'Have you a light?' He went to the mantelpiece to get a box of matches. 'I'm so sorry,' apologised Iris, 'I never asked you to have a cigarette.'

She held the case towards him, and he accepted one.

'When did you arrive?' asked Iris presently, as the smoke from their cigarettes floated gently upwards.

'About seven. And you?'

'I came through yesterday, from Glasgow. Dreadful journey. It's the first time I've been to Scotland. I can't say I'm fond of it.'

'It's really the wrong time of year, of course.'

'Yes, darling, but it's so barren.'

'There are worse places,' smiled Temple.

'How long are you staying here?' asked Iris.

'We thought of leaving tomorrow morning.'

'You're very wise. It's such awful weather, isn't it?'

'Frightful,' agreed Temple politely, wondering if she would ever come to the point.

'Did you write to Seaman about the play?' she questioned.

'Yes, he was quite decent about it all.'

'Oh, good. The play should stand a much better chance later in the year. Don't you think so?'

'Probably,' replied Temple in non-committal tones. He was not paying very much attention to her, for he imagined that he had a headache coming on. And he dreaded these very rare bouts of migraine. Then he realised that Iris' tone had changed. It was hard and determined . . . she might almost be playing a part.

'Temple, you know what I've come for, don't you?' she was saying, though he could not see her very clearly.

There seemed to be a lot of smoke from the two cigarettes.

'Yes, Iris, I know what you've come for.' His voice sounded rather distant, almost as if he were a ventriloquist and . . .

'I want that letter, and I want it now,' snapped Iris.

'Do you, Iris?' His voice sounded even more faint now. 'If the letter is of such . . . such . . .' He found he had difficulty in speaking. The smoke was much thicker now, almost like a smoke screen.

'What's the matter?' came Iris' cool voice.

'I—I don't know. My head—it's going round!' gasped Temple. 'My God, what have you done? There's a noise throbbing like—like—' He tottered towards a chair.

'Feeling sleepy?'

'What is it? What have you . . . done?'

'The cigarette,' said Iris quietly.

Those were the last words he heard. He staggered over to the window, but crashed against the table, and measured his length on the floor, bringing the coffee service on top of him.

In a flash, Iris began examining his pockets. She rapidly sifted through a small pile of letters. Threw aside his driving licence and insurance certificate. Made a brief search of his wallet. Hastily, she looked at the letters again . . .

She did not notice that the door had opened, and was badly scared when a polite voice interrupted her.

'You seem to be looking for something, madam. Can I be of any assistance?'

'Who the devil are you!' she cried in mingled surprise and anger.

The elderly man who stood in the doorway smiled. 'Permit me to introduce myself,' he said. 'My name is Steiner. Dr Ludwig Steiner.'

CHAPTER III

Instructions for a Murder

1

For some moments the silence was broken only by the rather abrupt ticking of a clock on the mantelpiece. Then Iris stood up, her little black evening bag in her left hand.

'What do you want?' she demanded jerkily.

Steiner hesitated, his hand still on the doorknob.

'I came to see Mr Temple,' he announced, 'but it appears my visit was a little—premature.'

Iris suddenly dived into her handbag and produced the tiny revolver which had belonged to Noel Hammond earlier in the evening.

'Stand away from that door!' she commanded.

'I beg your pardon?'

Iris repeated the order in brisk tones.

'I trust that revolver is not loaded, madam,' murmured Steiner rather nervously.

'Unless you do as I say,' she threatened, 'you will have an opportunity of finding out.'

Steiner moved cautiously into the room, following the beckoning revolver barrel.

'What is the matter with Mr Temple?' he asked, peering at the novelist's inert form.

'He's not feeling so good,' replied Iris sharply. 'Now – get over into that corner.'

'But surely you—' Steiner was beginning to protest, when she cut in again.

'Get—over—in—the—corner!' she commanded viciously, moving the revolver a few inches towards him.

'All right, if you insist,' replied Steiner in some alarm.

At her instruction, he moved into the corner farthest from the door. Iris relaxed for a moment, and thoughtfully surveyed the man on the floor. 'Nothing in his pockets,' she reflected in a whisper.

'What is it you are looking for?' asked Steiner, still obviously overcome with curiosity, in spite of her threatening attitude. The actress looked up and shot a piercing glance at him.

'What did you say your name was?' she demanded suddenly.

'Steiner. Dr Ludwig Steiner.'

'H'm . . . Is Temple a friend of yours?'

'Madam, Mr Temple looks rather ill,' said Steiner anxiously. 'I beg of you, let us—'

While he was making this protest Iris had moved swiftly over to the door. 'He's all yours, Doctor. He's all yours!' she said with a short laugh as she quickly opened the door and vanished along the corridor.

Steiner hardly waited until the door had closed before crossing to the unconscious novelist.

'Mr Temple . . . what's the matter . . . what's wrong?'

He shook Temple's shoulders vigorously for some time before the novelist showed any sign of returning life. Then

Temple stirred a little, half-opened his eyes, and passed a weary hand over his forehead.

'My God . . . my head's terrible!' he gasped.

'Don't try to get up,' advised Steiner, as Temple began to struggle to a sitting position. But the events of the past half-hour had now returned to Temple's memory, and he was obviously restless. When Steiner eventually managed to help him into a chair, Temple looked round the room in a dazed fashion.

'She's—gone?' he whispered at length.

'Yes, she's gone,' agreed Steiner soothingly. Temple made an effort to get to his feet, but the Austrian forced him back into the chair. 'Stay where you are,' he murmured, 'I'll get you a cushion.'

'I'll be all right in a minute,' said Temple, resting his throbbing head in his hands.

'Perhaps a drink—' Steiner began to suggest.

Temple shook his head. 'I'll be all right presently,' he announced. The fumes were already beginning to disperse. Steiner opened the window, and great gusts of air swirled into the room.

Suddenly there were footsteps outside, and Steve came in, followed by Sir Graham. She saw at a glance that Temple was not well.

'Paul—what's the matter?' she cried in alarm.

Temple forced a smile.

'It's—it's nothing, dear.'

'You look done in, Temple,' said Forbes in some concern. 'What the devil has happened?'

'After you left, Iris came here . . . she was looking for the letter,' he told them. 'Like a damned fool, I accepted a cigarette from her . . . and . . .' His voice trailed off.

'Take it easy, old man,' advised Forbes anxiously.

Steve looked round and noticed Steiner, who was standing over by the window. She turned towards the Chief Commissioner.

'This is Dr Steiner . . .

Forbes surveyed him shrewdly, as Steiner moved a little in their direction.

'I—I came here just to say "hello", Mrs Temple,' began Steiner nervously. 'I was feeling a little lonely. When I opened the door, I saw that Mr Temple was ill, and that a strange woman—'

'How long ago is this?' broke in Forbes briskly.

'But . . . just a moment ago . . .'

'Wait here,' Forbes bade the others, as he went to the door.

'It's no use,' said Steve quietly, and Forbes halted and half-turned.

'What do you mean?'

'Iris has gone,' Steve told him. 'Her car was outside before we went downstairs. Now it's disappeared. Look . . . you can see from the window,' she said, pointing. Then she returned to her husband. 'Are you feeling any better, darling?'

'Yes . . . I'm not so bad now,' he smiled up at her.

'You were saying, Dr Steiner . . . ?' Forbes quietly returned to the subject.

'I found a strange woman searching Mr Temple's pockets,' said Steiner eagerly. 'I did not know what to do – I was perplexed. Suddenly the lady in question produced a revolver, so I am afraid my actions became somewhat restricted, and alas – uninspired.'

'I'm beginning to think it's a damned good job you turned up,' put in Temple. 'That young lady meant business. She might have finished me off.'

'But what was she looking for?' demanded Steiner, obviously mystified.

'A letter,' answered Forbes.

'A letter!' echoed Steiner. 'It must have been very important.'

'Most important,' said Forbes softly. As no further information was offered, Steiner shrugged his shoulders.

'Mrs Temple, I was hoping that you and your husband might join me in a nightcap. . . Perhaps under the circumstances, however. . .'

Steve smiled.

'Thank you, Doctor. But I think perhaps it would be better if Paul went quietly to bed.'

'Of course, of course!' Steiner agreed at once. 'Good night, Mr Temple. I hope we shall meet again before we leave . . . Good night, sir!' He bowed politely to Forbes, who nodded curtly, and Steve saw him to the door. When it had closed behind the doctor's sturdy figure Temple sighed.

'I'm feeling much better now,' he decided.

'I should take it easy for a little while, dear,' Steve advised.

'Yes, all right,' he acquiesced, sinking into his chair. 'Oh, by the way, who wanted you on the telephone?'

'I don't know,' replied Steve doubtfully. 'There was a woman at the other end . . . she kept me waiting for ages, and then finally mumbled something about a wrong number. All the same, I'm pretty sure it wasn't a trunk call,' she added thoughtfully.

'The call was a fake – probably from a local box,' declared Forbes. 'They obviously wanted Steve out of the way while Iris did her stuff.'

'Yes, that would be it,' Temple agreed after a pause. 'We ought to have guessed that.' He pondered awhile before asking: 'Did you get in touch with Major Foster, Sir Graham?'

'Yes, I got in touch with Foster all right,' said Forbes grimly. Temple looked up suspiciously.

'What's the matter?' he demanded.

'We're in a spot, Temple,' said Forbes flatly. 'A devil of a spot. And we need your help. I'm sorry about Steve, because I know how she feels, but things are serious—damned serious.'

'What did Foster say?' asked Temple.

'If Hardwick is on the right track – and according to Noel Hammond's report he most certainly is – then it's absolutely imperative that we get Hardwick away from Skerry Lodge.'

'Yes,' murmured Temple, 'I agree with you.' His brain was beginning to function again.

'But surely Noel Hammond *is* at Skerry Lodge,' Steve pointed out.

'Even if Hammond is alive,' replied Forbes quietly, 'which I very much doubt, he's not likely to be at Skerry Lodge.'

'I don't understand,' said Steve.

'Sir Graham means that since they know about the letter they must obviously know that Hammond – or David Lindsay as they call him – is a British Agent.'

'Oh yes,' she agreed. 'I see that. But who exactly were those men who stopped us on the road?'

'One was Laurence van Draper,' said Forbes, 'and the other who called himself Lindsay was a gentleman by the name of Major Guest.'

'Then you know these people?' exclaimed Steve in some surprise.

'Oh yes, we know them all right. The Intelligence people know every member of the organisation, with the unfortunate exception of Z.4 . . . the one person who really matters.'

'But if the Secret Service know these people, why on earth don't they do something about it?'

'Well, for several reasons, Steve,' said Forbes. 'You see, first of all you must realise that we are not up against a criminal organisation. These people are a vastly different proposition from the Front Page Men, for instance. Most of them are well educated, and to all intents and purposes, at any rate, thoroughly respectable. Take Iris Archer, for example – a well-known West End actress . . . Laurence van Draper – probably the most celebrated philatelist in Europe.'

'I thought his name was familiar,' said Temple, taking a cigarette from his case and abruptly putting it back again.

'Then there's Major Guest,' Forbes pursued. 'He knows more about the Prenz machine gun than any man living.'

'Yes, I've read about that,' said Steve, 'but if these people are so respectable, then—'

'Just a minute, Steve,' interrupted Forbes. 'I didn't say they were respectable. I said – to all intents and purposes – they *appear* respectable. I think you will agree that there is a slight difference.'

He took a small notebook from his inside pocket.

'All the same,' Steve persisted, 'if these people are so well known, there must be some reason why they are willing to risk their reputations and—'

'Yes, that's true enough, Sir Graham,' Temple supported her. 'You said yourself that they represented no particular country, and since that seems automatically to wipe out any political factor—'

'It doesn't wipe out blackmail,' Forbes quietly pointed out.

'Blackmail!' echoed Steve.

'What do you mean?' demanded Temple.

Forbes turned over the pages of his notebook rather impatiently.

'Z.4 – whoever he or she may be – knows something incriminating about each member of the organisation. Of that I am sure,' he declared confidently.

'What makes you so certain?'

'Do you remember Janet O'Donnell?'

'The Irish poet?' queried Temple. 'She committed suicide, didn't she?'

Paul Temple recalled meeting Janet O'Donnell at a studio party in Chelsea, where she had recited some of her poems in that rich wailing brogue which had greatly intrigued him at the time. She had very dark, almost bluish tinted hair, brushed close to her head, and large luminous eyes that smouldered dimly as she recounted the sorrows of her race. Temple had felt that there was something tragic about her life, some great trouble deep down that surged and throbbed within her, finding occasional relief in her poems. He had always told himself that he would never forget that face. When he saw it on the front page of his newspaper one morning he instinctively knew what had happened. He could never imagine Janet O'Donnell dying a natural death.

'Yes, she preferred suicide to being a member of Z.4's organisation,' Forbes was saying.

Temple shivered slightly. Tragedy had been written in every line of the Irish girl's face, but all the same . . .

'You mean that Z.4 was blackmailing—' Steve was anxious to know.

'Exactly,' said Forbes. 'But Z.4 isn't a fool. Make no mistake about that. The people are paid well. The black-mailing side of the business merely ensures their loyalty.'

Temple's mind had been wandering slightly. 'I can't quite see why Hammond, or Lindsay, was working with Hardwick,' he murmured in mystification.

'Hammond was a research chemist,' expounded Forbes. 'A very brilliant one, too. Z.4 obviously discovered this, and made use of the fact.' He returned to his close perusal of the letter from Hammond, which he had taken from between the pages of his notebook.

'My God, I don't like the sound of this letter, Temple,' he growled. ' . . . Screen of definite value and importance. . . beam almost perfected . . .' He paced restlessly across the room.

'Whatever happens, we must get Hardwick away from Skerry Lodge!'

'Where is this lodge?' asked Temple.

'About four miles away – it's on the other side of High Moorford.'

Temple nodded thoughtfully. He recalled seeing the name on an ordnance map.

'Sir Graham, who do you think stole that letter?' asked Steve.

Forbes pursed his lips and frowned slightly.

'Well, quite candidly, I was inclined to think Dr Steiner – he seems a rum sort of bird. But if Steiner is a member of the organisation – or Z.4 himself for that matter – why should he return the letter?'

He placed the letter in question inside his notebook, just as a knock came at the door. It was Mrs Weston, who wanted to know if she could take away the coffee things.

'I'm afraid we've had a bit of an accident – one of the cups broken – I'm so sorry,' said Steve.

'That's all right, ma'am – these things do happen,' smiled Mrs Weston, busily collecting the bits.

Steve turned to her husband. 'Would you like anything to drink, darling?'

'Yes, I think I'll have a brandy and soda,' decided Temple. 'What about you?'

Forbes shook his head.

'One brandy and soda, sir?' repeated Mrs Weston, picking up the tray. 'Shocking weather, isn't it?'

'Does it always rain like this in Scotland?' demanded Steve conversationally.

'All the time I've been here – straight down and as wet as the devil,' chuckled Mrs Weston. 'I'll send your drink up right away, sir.'

When Mrs Weston had retreated, Forbes resumed his restless pacing.

'Temple, there's something I want to say to you,' he began quietly. 'And it's not going to be easy.'

'I think I know what it is, Sir Graham,' replied Temple with a short laugh. 'But don't worry, we're leaving in the morning.'

'That's just the point,' snapped Forbes. 'I don't want you to leave. Steve will have to go – that's imperative. But I need your help, Temple. Need it more than ever in my life before.'

Temple looked up questioningly.

'When I came up here, the Intelligence people told me my task would be a difficult one,' Forbes proceeded, 'and that I could use whatever means I thought fit, providing I succeeded.'

He paused for a moment, then declared grimly: 'I've got to get Z.4, Temple. No matter what happens, I've got to get Z.4!' He thumped the little table to emphasise the urgency of his words.

'And where exactly do I come in?' demanded Temple softly.

'Well. . .' temporised the Chief Commissioner, 'you've met van Draper and Major Guest and—'

'Isn't there another reason, Sir Graham?' insisted Temple with a slight smile.

'Yes,' agreed Forbes after a pause. 'The people we are up against are now pretty certain that you are Richmond – the man Hammond's letter was intended for.'

'M'm . . .' mused Temple. 'I'm not so sure about that.'

'And why do you want to get rid of me, Sir Graham?' asked Steve.

Forbes became even more serious. 'Things are too risky,' he declared flatly. 'In spite of their – what shall I call it? – veneer of respectability, these people are damnably dangerous.'

'He's right, darling,' nodded Temple, feeling that he had by no means got over the shock of his recent adventure.

Steve looked from one to the other and sighed. 'All right,' she finally agreed. 'You can run me over to Aberdeen in the morning. I believe there's a train at 12.10.' She wrinkled her forehead in thought. 'I'll go down to Bramley Lodge for a few days.'

'Yes—all right, Steve.' At that moment Ernie Weston came in, carrying a solitary glass of amber fluid on a tray.

'One brandy and ginger ale,' he announced.

'I asked for a brandy and soda,' Temple pointed out.

'Oh—sorry, guv'nor, I'll go and—' He started for the door, but Temple recalled him. 'That's all right. Put it down here.' Temple indicated the table.

'Yes, sir,' said Ernie, complying briskly.

Temple handed him a tip. 'Oh, by the way,' he said in friendly tones, 'I lost a cigarette lighter this evening after dinner. I was wondering if you had seen it or not?'

'No, not me, guv'nor,' replied Ernie promptly, a gleam of suspicion in his pale blue eyes.

'It's rather a good one,' continued Temple firmly, 'and I should hate to lose it permanently.'

Ernie's suspicion was immediately mixed with defiance.

'I 'aven't seen no lighter – 'onest I 'aven't,' he protested hoarsely. 'I don't know if you think as 'ow there's any funny business goin' on 'ere, but—'

'It's all right,' interrupted Temple mildly. 'I was just wondering, that's all. Good night.' His decisive manner obviously meant the incident was closed and called for no further discussion.

Ernie shuffled out rather self-consciously with a mumbled 'Good night.'

'Funny little devil,' commented Forbes with a half-smile. 'Nice to hear a bit of cockney, though, way up here.'

'Darling, I didn't know you'd lost your lighter,' said Steve quickly.

'I haven't,' murmured Temple imperturbably.

Before Steve could cross-question him there was a swift knock at the door. It was opened almost immediately to reveal the mackintosh-clad figure of Rex Bryant, his shabby felt hat in one hand, an unsmoked cigarette drooping from his lower lip.

'Why, Bryant! What the devil are you doing here?' cried Temple in amazement.

'Rex – this is a surprise!' supplemented Steve.

'Reporters do get about occasionally, you know,' Rex reminded them. 'I once even went as far as Southampton to interview a novelist who had just landed on the *Golden Clipper*. . . but that's another story, as the subeditor said.' He suddenly caught sight of Forbes, who had been standing in the background. 'Hello, Sir Graham, I didn't recognise you for a minute . . .' As he spoke, Temple went over to the doorway and closed the door.

'This is Rex Bryant – Sir Graham Forbes,' said Steve.

'And what is Mr Bryant of the London *Evening Post* doing in Scotland?' asked Forbes.

'Well, it's rather a long story. The editor got sarcastic – I got sarcastic. The editor got fresh – I got fresh. The editor got angry – I got—'

'The sack,' guessed Steve, who knew something of editors and their methods.

Rex shook his head. 'Not exactly. In point of fact, I resigned. But it was a very close race; my tongue works a bit faster than his.' He paused and eyed the novelist shrewdly up and down. 'You look a bit off colour, Temple,' he said.

'I'm all right,' replied Temple. 'But you still haven't told us why you came to Scotland.'

'To see the bluebells,' answered Rex, without a flicker of an eyelid. 'Incidentally, I got a bit of a shock when I spotted your name in the register.'

'In the register?' repeated Temple quietly. 'Oh yes . . . Well I think it might be a good idea if we all went downstairs and had a drink. What do you say?'

'Why not?' cried Rex gaily. 'Why not?'

On the way down, Paul Temple noticed that Rex Bryant was smiling. It was not the smile of a man who had just lost his job.

2

Built on a lavish plan by a wealthy American, Skerry Lodge seemed out of keeping with the sombre hills which surrounded it. Only a section of the house appeared to be in use, and several of the windows, even at the front, were half-covered with whitening. The outside of the house had obviously not been painted for some years, and had a decayed appearance which would have depressed its first owner. But it was well built, and continued to present a stolid aspect to the many Highland storms.

It stood in a cleft in the hills, and there was no other house in sight; in fact the nearest was at High Moorford, a mile and a half away.

In the drawing room of Skerry Lodge, Major Guest sat deep in an armchair, gloomily pondering upon the events of the past few days. He was a close student of both the novels and the exploits of Paul Temple, and the latter's incursion into the present situation had put the Major's nerves on edge. Paul Temple seemed to have such an uncanny knack of penetrating into the deepest laid plans, he reflected. It might be worth any risk to put him safely out of the way.

Outside, he could hear the voice of van Draper, speaking on the telephone in the gloomy hall. Eventually, van Draper came in.

'Any news of Iris?' asked Guest.

'No,' replied the other irritably, kicking a small rug out of his path as he strode to the fire. 'I feel like a drink,' he declared. 'Ring for Ben.'

Guest lazily stretched out an arm and pressed the bell.

'I've been thinking, Van. Suppose Temple doesn't happen to be Richmond, and he's passed on that letter.'

'Well, in that case it's all over,' snapped van Draper, 'so far as the letter is concerned, at any rate.'

Guest nodded. 'What do you think was in the letter?' he asked.

'I don't know,' thoughtfully replied van Draper. 'Although we can be certain of one thing.'

'What's that?'

'Hammond discovered that Hardwick's beam wasn't such a washout after all. That meant, of course, that the screen could be of some use to the War Office. And consequently—'

'Consequently the Intelligence people are going to swoop down on Skerry Lodge like—like—' Words evaded him for a moment. 'Well, anyhow, they're going to swoop down on us, and pretty soon too if you want my opinion.'

'Assuming, of course, that the letter reaches Richmond,' van Draper pointed out.

'But even if it doesn't – or at any rate hasn't,' persisted Guest, 'we still have Temple to contend with.'

Van Draper detected a note of fear in the other's voice, and eyed him rather contemptuously. 'That rather depends, doesn't it, on whether or not Iris succeeded?' he queried.

Heavy footsteps sounded outside, and the door opened to admit Ben. Ben Collins, assisted by a daily woman, made a sketchy attempt at running the domestic arrangements at Skerry Lodge. He was a rather heavily built man of about forty-five.

'Did you ring?' he asked in a deep, hoarse voice.

'Yes,' replied van Draper swiftly. 'Fetch me a whisky and soda.'

Ben crossed to the sideboard as if he resented the fact that van Draper could not get himself a drink. 'You haven't heard from Z.2 yet?' he asked.

'No. We're expecting her at any minute.'

'If she hasn't got that letter, we ought to get Hardwick and the screen out of here damn' quick, if you ask me,' said Ben.

'Yes, that's what I say,' agreed Guest quickly.

'We can't do that,' snapped van Draper. 'Not when we are expecting Z.4.'

'Do you think Z.4 really will come into the open this time?' It was Ben who spoke, and there was a note of irritation in his voice.

'He's got to.'

'But Hardwick's more or less finished working on the screen,' argued Guest. 'We're all set – so what the devil is he waiting—'

'Listen!' said Ben suddenly.

They were silent. In the distance the roar of a car could be heard, making its uncertain way along the rough and bumpy road that led to Skerry Lodge.

'Iris!' breathed Guest. 'She's certainly stepping on it.'

The car came flying to the front door and lurched itself to a stop. As Iris came into the room, the three men were standing anxiously awaiting her.

'What happened?' said Guest, almost as soon as she had opened the door. Iris dropped her bag on the table and perched herself rather wearily on the arm of a chair.

'Temple hasn't got the letter,' she announced. 'What's more, he isn't Richmond.'

'Then who is?'

'I don't know,' replied Iris in a depressed voice.

'What happened to Temple?' asked van Draper, tossing down the remains of his whisky.

Both Guest and van Draper were eyeing her anxiously. After a brief pause, she answered their unspoken query with a shake of the head. 'No. I used one of the cigarettes. It's no use putting Temple out of the way unless he intends to meddle.'

Guest seemed anxious to argue, but he was interrupted by the unexpected entrance of Mrs Moffat, heavily muffled in a plain grey woollen cloak. Ben was obviously startled, for Mrs Moffat never visited Skerry Lodge unless she had a particularly good reason for doing so.

'Mrs Moffat – what is it?' cried van Draper, in some alarm.

'You shouldn't have come here,' said Guest, rising to his feet.

Mrs Moffat was unperturbed. She crossed to the fireplace, threw back her cloak and announced: 'I've had my instructions from Z.4.' Her voice was quiet and unemotional. The men looked at each other. Curiosity mingled with a certain amount of apprehension.

'What are they?' asked van Draper at length.

Mrs Moffat folded her hands and surveyed them equably.

'Paul Temple and his wife leave for Aberdeen tomorrow morning – by road,' she informed them.

'Well?' said Guest.

Mrs Moffat gazed thoughtfully into the fire. 'They mustn't reach Aberdeen alive. That's all.'

There was silence for some moments.

'But how the devil can we stop them?' burst out Guest.

Ben, who had poured himself a generous drink, came over from the sideboard. 'There's a bridge, isn't there – not far from Skellyfore,' he murmured.

'A bridge?' repeated van Draper in puzzled tones. 'What the devil has a bridge got to do with it?'

Ben took a gulp of whisky. 'Have you ever been to Aberdeen by road from Inverdale?' he asked.

'No,' admitted van Draper, 'I haven't.'

Ben perched on the edge of the table and hugged his glass, 'There's a bridge about two miles from a village called Skellyfore,' he explained hoarsely. 'Just over the bridge is a corner – "Hell's Elbow", I think they call it. One of the worst

75

corners you've ever come across. They've got a big "Danger" sign that hits you slap in the eye just as you come to the bridge.' He paused, then added with a significant wink: 'Now if that "Danger" sign got lost somehow, and there was a car parked on the bend . . .'

'That's a damn' good idea!' broke in van Draper approvingly.

'Yes,' admitted Guest, 'but it might not be fatal.'

But Ben was equal to the emergency.

'It would be fatal all right,' he grunted, 'if there was something in the stationary car.'

Iris looked up in quick interrogation.

'You mean—an explosive!' cried van Draper. 'So that when Temple's car hits the other . . . my God, Ben, that's an idea! That's certainly an idea!'

'Ben, I didn't think you'd got the brain,' said Iris.

Ben grinned rather sheepishly and poured himself another drink.

Meanwhile, the Major turned to Mrs Moffat and began to question her about the instructions she had received. He was mystified to think that Z.4 should prefer to communicate them to this dour little Scotswoman rather than to himself or van Draper. Mrs Moffat dived into a shabby handbag and produced a slip of paper, which she handed to Guest. On it was typewritten:

Paul Temple and wife motoring to Aberdeen tomorrow morning. Imperative that they do not reach there.

Guest passed it round without a word.

Van Draper glanced at it casually, then said: 'I wonder how Z.4 knew about Temple leaving for Aberdeen.'

Guest shrugged his shoulders. 'The note seems to suggest that Z.4 must be staying at the inn, doesn't it?' he hazarded.

'Yes,' reflected Guest. 'That's true.' He folded the note thoughtfully and gave it to Iris.

Ben took advantage of their absorption to help himself to yet another large drink.

3

Paul Temple rather enjoyed driving along these Highland roads with their sudden bends and steep gradients. He liked to nurse the car, to get the most out of her in the struggle to overcome these obstacles which had yet to succumb completely to the hand of Man.

Temple and Steve had started out soon after breakfast, following quite a touching farewell between Steve and Mrs Weston, who had apparently 'taken a reet fancy' to her visitor. They had previously explained to the Westons that Steve's telephone message had been an urgent recall to a sick relative in London, and both host and hostess had been suitably sympathetic, though this morning Mrs Weston had displayed a somewhat embarrassing curiosity.

However, that was all over now, and the car had been purring to Temple's satisfaction for the past hour. The roads were not yet dry after the previous night's rain, and once or twice Temple had to correct a slight skid.

At length they came to the tiny village, which a huge black and gold sign indicated as Skellyfore, adding that Aberdeen was forty-two miles distant. As her husband slowed down a little to pass through the village, Steve took advantage of the rather more subdued roar of the engine to start a conversation.

'Paul,' she began gently.

'Yes, darling?'

'You—you will take care of yourself, won't you?' she demanded in rather a shaky voice.

Temple grinned.

'Of course I will,' he assured her cheerily. 'Good heavens, Steve, there's nothing to worry about!'

Steve wasn't so sure. Although she was accustomed by now to Temple extricating himself from a series of complicated situations, the events of the past two days seemed far more formidable than anything he had previously tackled.

After a long pause, she asked: 'Why do you think Rex Bryant came to Inverdale?'

'I haven't the faintest idea,' replied Temple, swerving skilfully to avoid an ancient hen which had chosen that particular moment to cross the road.

'His story about getting the sack didn't sound very convincing, did it?' persisted Steve.

'Oh, I don't know,' smiled Temple, still refusing to be drawn.

Steve tried another line of approach.

'Paul, I rather think Sir Graham suspects Dr Steiner.'

'Dr Steiner . . . 'm . . .' murmured Temple dubiously.

'What exactly does that mean?'

Temple turned and smiled at her.

'Amongst other things, it means that Steiner was right about the hotel register.'

'You mean that you did sign it after all?'

'No. The landlord brought a new one out for the doctor to sign and added a few names from the old register – including ours.'

Steve wrinkled her forehead in deep thought. Her thoughts were interrupted, however, by three strident hoots from a bright red sports car which was rapidly gaining on them.

'Then Dr Steiner really did see our names—' she was beginning, when the hooting became more insistent.

'Pull over, darling. There's a car wants to pass!'

Temple peered into the driving mirror, then at the narrow road ahead.

'He can't pass me here,' he replied. 'It's much too narrow. Besides, there's a bridge ahead of us.'

But the other car was on their tail now, still hooting away. The small stone bridge ahead was only just wide enough to accommodate a fair-sized lorry, and certainly would not permit one car to pass another. On the other side of the bridge the road seemed to disappear, though it actually wound round a hairpin bend to reappear on the far side of a ravine.

'Let him pass before we get to the bridge,' cried Steve, who was all for giving way on the road.

'Don't be silly. Why should I?' smiled her husband, always a driver who insisted on his rights. However, two hundred yards in front of the bridge the road widened appreciably for a short distance, and when Steve once more urged him to slow down, he obliged.

'All right – anything to be rid of that dreadful horn,' said Temple. 'Come on – road hog!'

The road hog came.

He was a youngish man, with a rather pleasant smile, and he gave three polite hoots by way of acknowledgment as he shot past.

'After all,' said Steve, 'he might be a doctor on the way to a serious case.'

'He's certainly in a hurry to get somewhere,' agreed Temple, as the car seemed to bounce over the slightly humpbacked bridge and out of sight. When they were about fifty yards away, Temple suddenly gave vent to an exclamation.

'My God! – there's a corner on the other side of the bridge!' he cried, clapping on both brakes. As they came to the bridge, they were just in time to see the sports car heading full tilt for a massive old Buick which had been parked on the bend. The driver had the alternative of colliding with it or turning off the road and hurtling down the ravine. The brakes screamed, but the car must have been travelling at quite forty miles an hour when it hit the stationary vehicle.

Almost instantaneously there was an explosion and both cars seemed to be enveloped in a sheet of flame.

'Come along, Steve!' shouted Temple, jumping out of his car and running towards the scene of the accident.

But they were compelled to stop quite ten yards short of the burning cars. The heat was both intense and unexpected. Temple took his wife's arm to prevent her going nearer. He was afraid that there might be yet another explosion from one of the petrol tanks.

'Oh, Paul . . . poor fellow . . . it's terrible . . . !'

'There's nothing we can do,' he told her gently.

'But who left the car in such a position . . . and on this dreadful corner? It was madness!' she cried.

He looked at her for a moment, then his hand closed over hers.

'It was meant for us, Steve,' he said gently.

'For us?' repeated Steve, a look of horror in her eyes, as the truth dawned upon her. Temple walked as near as he could to the burning cars, then turned and rejoined his wife.

'Come along, darling,' he said. 'We're going back to Inverdale.'

4

After Paul Temple had left the inn, Sir Graham Forbes had taken a short stroll over the moors, smoking two pipes of his favourite tobacco in the process. No doubt Temple would have some bright ideas on his return, he consoled himself. He was strongly tempted to reconnoitre in the direction of Skerry Lodge, but decided that this procedure had better be postponed until he had someone to take with him.

He had noticed Rex Bryant returning from that direction earlier in the morning, but attached little importance to the fact. After all, he reflected, there were only two roads out of Inverdale, and anyone out for exercise was bound to use one of them. Rex had been full of high spirits, and had spent some minutes with Sir Graham, inquiring after various members of the New Scotland Yard personnel, with whom he seemed quite familiar.

When he arrived back at the inn, Sir Graham decided that it would be in their mutual interest if he and Temple shared the same room, so he went in search of Mrs Weston to make the necessary arrangements. He found her in the private sitting room, which also served as an office. She was dabbing at her eyes with an untidy apron and shaking with suppressed sobs.

'Hullo, Mrs Weston, is there some trouble?' began Forbes. She turned quickly and looked up at him.

'Oh, it's you, Mr Richmond. I didn't hear you come in.'

'Can I help at all?' asked Forbes in his serious tones.

'It's . . . it's Ernie!' she burst out suddenly. 'He's . . . he's gone!'

'Come on, Mrs Weston, pull yourself together!' urged Forbes. 'He'll show up all right. He's probably met some friends or—'

'But I can't understand it,' sobbed Mrs Weston, bewilderment written in every line of her honest North Country features. 'He's never done this before. We've been married

81

for nigh on sixteen years and Ernie has never been away an hour without telling me. He was never one for that sort of thing – always liked his home comforts and . . . and . . .'

Her voice broke down completely.

'When was the last time you saw your husband?'

'Last night,' Mrs Weston told him. 'We'd locked up for the night, and was more or less getting ready for bed when Ernie suddenly said 'e'd take the dog for a walk. That was the last I ever . . .' Once more her voice trailed into sobs.

'What seems to be the matter?' came in a slightly guttural accent from the direction of the doorway. Forbes half-turned, realising that he must have left the door ajar, and that Mrs Weston's sobs must have attracted attention. Dr Steiner stood by the door, and Rex Bryant was peering over his shoulder.

'It's Mr Weston,' said Forbes briefly, not altogether relishing the interruption.

'Our respected host?' queried Steiner with a lift of the eyebrows. 'He is not ill, I trust?'

'Not exactly,' answered Forbes. 'But—he's disappeared.'

'Disappeared?' echoed Steiner. 'But that is impossible. I saw him last night. Why, he served me with my lager just before supper.'

'Yes, well, he hasn't been seen since,' retorted Forbes rather bluntly.

'So?' Steiner was obviously very taken aback.

Rex came into the room and perched himself on the corner of the table, swinging one leg easily, and looking vaguely interested.

'It wouldn't by any chance be that little cockney bloke who was here when I arrived?' he demanded in a casual tone.

Forbes nodded, then turned to Mrs Weston again.

'Mrs Weston, when your husband went for a walk, did he seem in a good humour? He wasn't worried by any chance?'

'Er—no—I don't think so,' she replied a little uncertainly. 'What time was it exactly – do you remember?'

'Well, as near as I can tell, about eleven.'

Rex Bryant edged off the table quite suddenly. 'You mean this fellow went out at eleven last night and hasn't been seen since?' He seemed very surprised at the news.

'How was he dressed?' pursued Forbes, intent on solving this minor mystery, which he somehow felt might well have a bearing on the main issue.

Mrs Weston thought for a moment. 'He had his blue serge trousers on – and an old sports jacket – and, I believe, a white muffler.'

Before she could recall any further details, the door was pushed open to admit Paul Temple and Steve.

'Hello, Temple,' said Forbes in rather absent-minded fashion. Then for the first time he saw Steve. 'Why, hello, Steve – I thought—'

Temple cut him short.

'I want to see you straight away – come to my room. Could I have the key, Mrs Weston? Number 172.'

Mrs Weston went across to the board where the keys hung, and Steiner seized the opportunity to speak to the newcomers.

'So you decided not to leave us after all, eh, Mrs Temple? That is good.'

But Steve was hardly listening. She had noticed Mrs Weston's swollen eyes. 'Is anything the matter, Mrs Weston?' she asked, for she had taken quite a fancy to the little North Country woman.

Mrs Weston did not reply, but pretended to busy herself searching for the key.

It was Forbes who answered her query. 'Mrs Weston is very upset.'

'What's the trouble?' asked Temple.

'Weston went out last night about eleven o'clock – and he hasn't been seen since.'

'You mean he's—disappeared?' cried Steve.

Forbes nodded.

'Oh, but that's impossible!' Temple placed a warning hand on his wife's shoulder. 'Don't worry, Mrs Weston. He'll turn up all right,' he murmured reassuringly.

'Thank you, sir,' said Mrs Weston, handing him the key.

'Coming, Steve?'

She caught the meaningful look from her husband.

'Let me carry that case, Steve,' offered Sir Graham, taking it from her.

'We shall see you both later, I hope?' suggested Dr Steiner.

'Why, yes, of course, Doctor,' smiled Steve, as she went out.

As Temple passed him, Rex Bryant placed a hand on his arm.

'I'd like to have a word with you, Temple, if I may.'

A little taken aback at this rather elaborate politeness, Temple paused. 'All right,' he agreed at length. 'Come to my room in about ten minutes.'

Temple did not address his companions as they walked out into the entrance hall and up the staircase. He unlocked the bedroom door with the somewhat cumbersome key.

'Put the case down anywhere, Sir Graham,' smiled Steve, going across to the dressing table and taking off her hat. Temple carefully closed the door.

'Temple, what on earth made you change your mind about going to Aberdeen? It must have been something—'

'Have you ever heard of "Hell's Elbow", Sir Graham?'

Forbes ruminated for a moment or two.

'Why, yes, it's that very bad corner about two miles from Skellyfore, isn't it?'

Temple nodded with a rather grim smile.

'Well, someone parked a car on the corner – and if a poor devil in a sports car hadn't tried to show off and . . .'

Temple's voice trailed away as he noticed Steve's rather startled expression.

'Look at the cupboard,' she said, in answer to his unspoken inquiry.

'What's the matter with it?'

'I mean . . . on the floor . . . there's some red paint or ink or something . . . it looks as if. . .'

Temple crossed to the cupboard and peered at the dark stain. 'That's not paint,' he murmured softly.

Forbes joined him and caught his breath in astonishment.

'We'd better open the door,' he decided, seizing the knob.

The door was obviously locked.

'Looks damn' queer,' said Forbes. 'We'll have to force it open, that's all.'

'Allow me,' said Temple, taking out a rather strong pocket-knife.

In two minutes he stood back and Forbes turned the knob. But the door had stuck, and it was not until he had wrenched it sharply that it jerked open, precipitating him backwards onto Temple.

A queer, inanimate form slumped out of the cupboard and fell to the floor. Steve shrieked in terror.

She had recognised the body of Ernie Weston.

Forbes and Temple bent over the body.

'He's dead all right,' said the latter, repressing a slight shudder. 'Almost instantaneous, I should think.'

'Oh, Paul, how horrible . . . how horrible!' gasped Steve, clutching the rail of the bed for support.

'Look out, she's going to faint!' snapped Forbes.

Temple rushed across to his wife and caught her arm.

'I'm all right,' she managed to smile weakly. But Temple insisted on leading her to a chair. Then he returned to Forbes, who was making a close survey of the dead man.

'There's something in his hand,' he pronounced at length, indicating a clenched fist. It was by no means easy to force apart the stiffened fingers, and some minutes had elapsed before Forbes produced a length of fairly fine gold chain. 'It looks to me like a watch chain,' he decided, rather dubiously.

'Let me see,' said Temple. 'Yes, it's a watch chain all right. I've seen it before somewhere, too . . .'

'Now you come to mention it, I think I've seen something like it,' said Forbes, his brow corrugated in an effort to remember.

Suddenly they realised that Steve had left the chair and was standing close behind them.

'That watch chain,' she cried excitedly. 'I know whose it is!'

'Steve, do calm yourself, darling,' begged Temple.

'But I know that chain – I've often noticed it.'

'Oh!' said Forbes, looking up sharply. 'Who does it belong to?'

Steve fingered the length of chain, as if to make quite certain before she spoke. Then she turned to Forbes.

'It belongs,' she said, 'to Rex Bryant.'

CHAPTER IV

Appointment with Danger

1

Almost automatically, Steve found herself dragging from the recesses of her subconscious mind various isolated facts about Rex Bryant. In her reporter days, Steve had been with him on one or two assignments, and, though they had worked for opposition papers, Rex had taken rather a fancy to her. Once or twice they had spent an odd half-hour over coffee while waiting for a story to materialise, and without much invitation he had told her various incidents in his lively career.

Like many Fleet Street reporters, Rex had graduated on a provincial paper, steadily ploughing through the inevitable routine of calls – police stations, vicarages, post offices, council offices and private houses. And like so many other reporters, he had rebelled after a time, and fled to Fleet Street to work on 'space'. Soon the paper discovered that this was rather an expensive proposition, so he was offered a weekly salary, which he promptly accepted.

At first he was given crime stories to cover, and within a few years had a highly specialised knowledge of the Metropolitan underworld. But his activities did not end there, and he created a minor sensation with a series of articles exposing what he blithely termed 'the political racket'; revealing that certain financiers were extremely anxious to keep several fingers in the Parliamentary pie. These articles resulted in a small crop of libel actions, but rather to everyone's surprise Rex and the *Evening Post* came through smiling.

Rex Bryant was no ordinary reporter. In spite of the news editor's attempts to suppress his irreverence for authority, he maintained his reputation as one of the few individuals who still bring the spirit of adventure to Fleet Street. On an average Rex was sacked about four times a year, but he was always reinstated after intervals varying from one hour to several weeks. If he was not re-engaged within a couple of days he made no effort to join another paper, though he would certainly have had little difficulty in doing so.

Yes, reflected Steve, she had found Rex Bryant extremely amusing, full of interesting information, and above all, very human.

Sir Graham was making a careful examination of the watch chain. 'It belongs to Bryant all right,' he murmured.

Temple knelt by the body and began to run through the various pockets. 'Nothing much here,' he announced after a while. Then suddenly he discovered a tiny fob pocket. 'Hello, what's this?' He held out a small platinum ring.

'Looks like a wedding ring,' said Forbes.

Temple nodded.

'Rather an expensive one,' commented Steve, taking a closer look.

'Now what the devil would Ernie Weston be doing with a platinum wedding ring?' demanded Forbes in some bewilderment.

'H'm . . . this rather bears out what I thought,' murmured Temple enigmatically.

'Sir Graham, you don't think Ernie Weston has anything to do with this other business?' asked Steve.

Forbes had to confess himself temporarily beaten. Temple continued his search through the dead man's pockets without discovering anything else of importance. He was interrupted by the arrival of Rex Bryant.

Rex came in, looking considerably more cheerful than he had on the previous evening. 'Sorry to barge in like this, old man,' he began blithely, then suddenly caught sight of the body at the far end of the room.

Forbes said quietly: 'It's Weston.'

Even the hard-boiled Rex was taken aback.

'My God! Is he dead?'

'Yes,' nodded Forbes grimly. 'He's dead.'

'But what happened?' demanded Rex. 'Where did he come from?' He looked at each of them in turn. 'Damn it all, don't stand there staring at me as if—' His eye suddenly caught the length of chain which Sir Graham was holding in his open palm. 'Where did you get that watch chain?' he asked in a different tone.

'You've seen it before?' said Sir Graham.

Rex said: 'Why of course I've seen it before. It's mine.'

'You don't deny it?' It was Steve who spoke, and there was a note of apprehension in her voice.

'Deny it? Of course I don't deny it. Why the devil should I?'

'When we found Weston,' Temple told him, 'he had that watch chain in his hand.'

'In his hand?'

'It rather looked as if there had been some sort of struggle,' Temple suggested.

Bryant's expression changed. He seemed rather taken off his guard.

'My God, Temple, you don't think I had anything to do with this?' he cried incredulously.

'The watch chain, Rex,' Temple pointed out suavely. 'It's evidence – rather important evidence, I should say.'

Rex seemed to realise the full force of this at once, and looked even more alarmed. 'I don't know whether this is some sort of joke, Temple! Good God, man, why should I kill Weston? I'd never even met the fellow before—before I came here.'

'And the watch chain?' persisted Forbes.

'I—I lost it,' said Rex. 'Last night after I got to bed I noticed it wasn't in my waistcoat.'

'Did you mention this to anyone?'

'No,' he decided. 'I thought it had slipped out – the fastening worked loose – they do sometimes.' Then another thought struck him. 'Yes, I did – I mentioned it to Dr Steiner. He was telling me about some gold cufflinks he'd lost, and we were wondering—'

'You were wondering what?'

'Well, as a matter of fact we thought the cufflinks and watch chain might have—got together.'

'You mean, you thought perhaps they'd both been stolen by the same person?' suggested Steve.

Rex nodded. 'And you can take it from me, Temple—' he was beginning with all his old assurance, but Temple interrupted him.

'I have my own ideas about this business, Rex. But I should like you to tell us why you came to Scotland in the first place.'

Rex obviously did not altogether relish this pertinent question. 'Why I came to Scotland?' he repeated slowly.

'Yes,' said Temple, motioning him to take a seat.

Rex perched on the arm of a chair, frowned thoughtfully for a few moments, then seemed to make up his mind.

'I came because of a man named Hardwick – John Hardwick,' he told them.

'Hardwick!' echoed Forbes in complete astonishment. 'What the devil do you know about Hardwick?'

Even Temple seemed a little surprised.

'About a week ago, Sir Graham, a man walked into the offices of the *Evening Post*. He was an untidy-looking individual, but in spite of his clothes he had a certain – what shall I say? – a certain "air" about him. He asked to see the news editor, but Cosgrove was in one of his "touch-me-not" moods, and he sent me out to have a chat with the fellow. He likes to unload that sort of job on me. Why, I could tell you things about Cosgrove that—'

'All right – go on with your story!' snapped Sir Graham.

'Well, as it happened, on this occasion the fellow told me a damned interesting story. First of all, he said his name was Hardwick – Hubert C. Hardwick, and that his brother, John Hardwick, had invented some sort of a smoke screen which, coupled with an invention known as the Inverdale Beam, would set the War Office all agog. Now I'd already heard of John Hardwick, and I knew for a fact that the War Office had turned down the invention because the Inverdale Beam had proved to be a failure.'

'Did Hubert Hardwick know this?' interrupted Temple.

'He did. But this is the extraordinary part about the business. Apparently, after the invention had been rejected, John Hardwick returned to Inverdale, and started work all over again on the beam. About two or three months later his brother – the chappie I saw – tried to get in touch with him, and rather to his surprise was unable to do so. He came up to Inverdale for two or three weeks in the hope of staying for a short while at Skerry Lodge, but he couldn't even get farther than the main gate. So, in desperation, he returned to London.'

'Is this Hubert C. Hardwick a wealthy man?' asked Forbes.

'Just the opposite. He hasn't a bean.'

Forbes nodded. 'Go on.'

'Well, there's very little more to tell, really,' continued Rex. 'Hubert Hardwick was convinced that his brother was being held a prisoner, and was hoping that we'd take the trouble to investigate the matter and pay him a pretty substantial sum for the privilege of doing so. The poor devil didn't know much about Fleet Street, I'm afraid,' he added with a short laugh.

'What did Cosgrove say to all this?' Steve was anxious to discover.

'You know Cosgrove as well as I do,' grinned Rex. 'I think he had some sort of idea that I'd made it all up. I tried to convince him that the story was well worth a break, but he wouldn't even listen. About two weeks later I got the sack.' Rex took a cigarette from his case and scratched a match. 'To be quite honest, Temple, it was the day after I saw you at Southampton. Naturally, I felt pretty despondent about things – I'd been on the London *Evening Post* for nearly ten years – and between me and you I made a pretty good attempt to liquidate my sorrows, as it were. Late that night, and purely by chance, I ran into Hubert C. Hardwick. I was pretty well sozzled by the time we met, and for the first couple of hours I don't believe I even realised who the devil he was. Anyhow, he'd been up to Inverdale since our first meeting, but he'd met with very little success. Skerry Lodge was guarded like Woolwich Arsenal. It was utterly impossible to get near the place. Well, to be brief, I got pretty curious. It seemed to me that a first-rate scoop was just sitting up waiting to be—'

'And so you came to Scotland,' interrupted Forbes.

'Exactly, Sir Graham.'

'Have you been near Skerry Lodge since you arrived here?' asked Temple.

'You bet your life,' snapped Rex briskly.

'What sort of place is it?'

'Looks more like a medieval castle than anything else. It's built on the side of a small lake in the hills – Loch Abaford I believe they call it.'

'Did you get near the house?'

'As a matter of fact, I didn't try,' Rex admitted. 'Hubert Hardwick's frontal attack had failed, so I decided to get the lie of the land before I did any real sightseeing.'

At this point Steve took Temple by the arm and said softly: 'Paul, don't you think one of us ought to see Mrs Weston and ...?'

'Yes, I've been thinking about that, Steve,' he replied. 'I think it might be a good idea if you broke the news. You seem to be able to handle her better than we do.'

Steve nodded, and quietly left them.

'Here's your watch chain, Bryant,' said Forbes at length. 'I should take better care of it in future.'

Rex seemed a little surprised to get the chain back.

'Look here, Sir Graham, I don't know whether you still think I had anything to do with this business, but I can assure you on my word of honour that—'

Temple did not seem unduly impressed by the reporter's obvious sincerity. He merely thrust the wedding ring in front of Rex and asked: 'Have you seen this before?'

'Why, no,' replied the reporter in a puzzled voice. 'What is it? Looks like a wedding ring.'

'Yes,' agreed Temple evenly. 'I should imagine that's what it is.'

Rex picked up the ring rather gingerly and examined it. 'Where did you get it?'

'We found it – on Weston,' Temple informed him.

Once again Rex seemed surprised.

Then Temple asked: 'What was it you wanted to see me about?'

Rex shifted rather uncomfortably. 'I think we'll leave that till later,' he said. 'It's not very important. . .'

Temple nodded.

'Then you might pop downstairs and see how Steve's getting on with Mrs Weston – she might want some help. I'm afraid it'll be a dreadful shock for the old girl.'

'All right,' agreed Rex, and after a moment's hesitation, made for the door.

When the door had closed, Forbes turned towards the novelist.

'This business is getting serious – damned serious,' he began urgently. 'We've got to get Hardwick away from Skerry Lodge – and above all we've got to get Z.4.'

Temple thoughtfully fingered the platinum ring.

'If John Hardwick has succeeded in perfecting the Inverdale Beam,' he mused, 'he'll have served his purpose . . . so far as Z.4 is concerned, at any rate.'

'Yes, but according to the letter we received from Lindsay, or rather Hammond, he hasn't perfected it. At least, not quite. We may still be in time, Temple.'

The novelist hardly seemed to be listening. With his hands thrust deep in his pockets, he stared for some moments out of the window. Then he turned.

'Have you got that letter, Sir Graham?'

'Yes,' answered Forbes, fumbling in his wallet and producing the letter in question.

Identity of Z.4 unknown even by important members of organisation. Believe Z.4 to be in Scotland and likely to contact headquarters within next three weeks.

Temple carefully refolded the note and handed it back to Sir Graham.

'Headquarters,' repeated Forbes with some deliberation. 'I wonder if Hammond meant Skerry Lodge.'

'I don't know,' Temple admitted. His brain was working in other directions. 'If the identity of Z.4 is unknown,' he propounded at length, 'then how will he contact the organisation? They must have some means of identification, or—'

'Z.4 has probably supplied them with some sort of password,' prompted Forbes, 'so that when he does contact them they will instantly recognise him – or her.'

Temple lifted his eyebrows at the suggestion implied in the Chief Commissioner's last two words. 'You don't think Iris Archer happens to be Z.4?'

Sir Graham merely smiled.

'Rather like a medieval castle . . . that's what Bryant said about Skerry Lodge, isn't it?' mused Temple. 'Sounds interesting. I think it might be quite a good idea if Steve and I drove over there.'

'For God's sake don't take any risks,' urged Forbes, and crossed over to the dead man. He eyed the body thoughtfully through half-closed eyes.

'Who do you think murdered him?'

'Z.4,' replied Temple coolly.

'But—why?' asked Forbes in some surprise.

'Exactly, Sir Graham. But—why?'

'You think Ernie Weston was a member of the organisation?'

'I'm almost sure he wasn't,' smiled Temple.

Forbes was obviously anxious to pump Temple further, but there was a faint knock at the door, which opened an inch or so. 'May I come in, Mr Temple?' came the familiar voice of Dr Steiner.

'Dr Steiner!' cried Temple. 'Why, yes, please do.'

Steiner closed the door rather clumsily. He was wearing a badly fitting suit of grey tweeds, and his tie was not quite straight. It was obvious that he was more than a little agitated.

'This is a dreadful business, is it not?' he began, taking one look at Weston and turning away with a shudder. 'I have just left Mrs Temple, she told me about . . . about this poor fellow.'

Temple manoeuvred him over to the fireplace.

'Dr Steiner,' he began earnestly, 'is it true that you lost a pair of cufflinks the night you arrived here?'

Steiner seemed to have expected a more urgent question.

'Why, yes—yes, that's true,' he declared. 'But why do you ask? Perhaps they have been found—yes?'

Temple shook his head. 'No. I'm afraid they haven't. But I think you'll get them back all right.'

'I hope so,' said Steiner. 'Indeed, I hope so.'

It was Sir Graham's turn to speak, and there was a glint in his grey eyes as he surveyed Steiner.

'Doctor Steiner, I wonder if you would permit me to ask you rather an unusual question?' he began.

After a short pause Steiner gave a slight shrug.

'But—of course.'

'What are you doing in Scotland?' queried Forbes in level tones.

'In Scotland?' repeated Steiner with a bewildered glance at Temple. 'Why . . . I am on holiday.'

'Perhaps it would be just as well if I introduced—' Temple began.

'My name is Richmond,' interposed Forbes. 'John Richmond.'

'And mine, sir, is Steiner – Doctor Ludwig Steiner,' declared the Austrian. 'Professor of Philosophy at the Unversity of Philadelphia.'

2

Ben Collins gave a cursory polish to some newly washed tumblers in the drawing room at Skerry Lodge. He was a big man, both in voice and manner, but he moved about the drawing room with a strange, almost feline dignity. His outward manner gave no indication of his real feelings, for beneath his calm and impersonal demeanour he was both nervous and apprehensive. According to plan, reflected Ben, the battered sports car at the foot of the ravine should have been Temple's. He felt intensely annoyed that his plan had not succeeded. And coupled with his annoyance he felt a strange foreboding. Once before a carefully laid plan had failed, and the outcome had not been pleasant. Ben shrugged his shoulders. It was a gesture he instinctively made when his thoughts wended their way into unpleasant channels. He did not like to think of Rita Allenby, nor of the single sheet of grey notepaper he had received after the inquest. He still had that sheet of notepaper tucked away in his wallet. The first, and only, communication he had personally received from Z.4.

The note had given a detailed account of his movements on the night of the murder, and had politely informed him that in his haste to escape from the somewhat sordid atmosphere of a Bloomsbury boarding house he had dropped a handkerchief. A handkerchief bearing both initials and laundry mark. Z.4 had assured him, however, that there was no danger of this information falling into the hands of the police, providing he obeyed instructions. Two days later Ben obeyed the instructions he had received, and for the first time was introduced to Laurence van Draper. At first he did not like van Draper. There was a certain 'air' about him, thought Ben, which immediately stamped him as a member of the leisured classes. He also had the unfortunate habit of asking a great many questions. Ben did not like men who asked questions; and he most certainly was not an admirer of what he flamboyantly termed 'proletarian enemies'. Also, Ben had a shrewd suspicion that van Draper might be Z.4. Later, however, when he became more intimately connected with the organisation, he revised his opinion on this matter and to a certain extent of van Draper himself.

Certainly both van Draper and Guest were annoyed that Temple had escaped, and each tried to blame the other for the mismanagement of the accident.

'You saw the car, Guest. Why the devil didn't you make some attempt to stop it?' van Draper was saying.

'Stop it?' laughed Guest sardonically. 'Don't talk such damned nonsense. The idiot must have been doing sixty.'

'Everything was fine,' said Ben from the sideboard. 'Even the weather played into our hands.'

'All right, all right,' said van Draper, rather resenting this from Ben. 'There's no need to start going into that all over again.'

'Not the slightest need,' said a cool, feminine voice.

Iris Archer stood in the doorway.

'Oh, so you're back,' said Guest, swinging round in his chair. 'What's happened about Temple?'

'He's back at the inn,' Iris informed him, drawing off her gloves. She went to the sideboard and helped herself to a whisky and soda, waving aside Ben's offer to mix it for her.

'The car idea wasn't so hot after all, eh, Ben?' She smiled grimly, setting down the glass.

'It would have been,' protested Ben indignantly, 'if that damn' fool of a driver hadn't stepped on it and got there first.'

'I'm beginning to think Temple is one of those lucky devils who can't be put out,' said Guest.

'If Temple is still at the inn, you'd better take care of him, Iris.'

Iris slowly shook her head.

'That's out of the question, Ben. I can't go back there – not now.'

'Of course she can't, Laurence.' Guest backed her up.

'Temple has got to be taken care of,' asserted van Draper, on the verge of losing his temper again. 'We've bungled one attempt, and we mustn't bungle another.'

'Indeed we mustn't,' said a quiet voice.

'Mrs Moffat!' cried van Draper.

Mrs Moffat closed the door and came towards the centre of the room. Mrs Moffat's visits to Skerry Lodge were very infrequent and her appearance filled the room with an air of expectancy.

'You've got to get Hardwick away,' she declared firmly.

'Why?' demanded van Draper in some surprise.

'What's happened?' supplemented Guest.

'My God!' gasped Ben. 'Don't say the police—'

Iris crossed over to Mrs Moffat. 'You've had instructions from Z.4?'

Mrs Moffat nodded.

'There's nothing to get alarmed about,' she announced, 'only we've got to get Hardwick and the screen away from Skerry Lodge.'

'But—why?' persisted van Draper softly.

'Because of Temple.'

'I don't understand,' he said, rather bewildered.

'Paul Temple,' Mrs Moffat slowly informed them, 'is coming here.'

Guest and van Draper exchanged startled glances.

'How do you know this?' It was van Draper who spoke.

'Instructions,' replied Mrs Moffat with a brief smile, 'from Z.4.'

'And what's going to happen?'

'Van Draper and Guest can take Hardwick down to the chalet,' decided Mrs Moffat. She turned towards Guest, who was helping himself to a drink. 'You must hold him there until you receive word from Ben.'

'And what,' demanded Ben, 'am I supposed to be doing while all this is going on?'

Mrs Moffat smiled again, a grim, twisted little smile that accentuated every line on her face.

'You will be entertaining Mr Temple,' she replied calmly.

'Entertaining Temple!' echoed Ben.

Mrs Moffat nodded with slow emphasis.

'When Temple arrives,' proceeded Mrs Moffat smoothly, 'you will show him in here, and then go down into the basement.'

'Basement?' said van Draper, obviously puzzled.

'My God!' cried Ben. 'You don't want me to flood the basement?'

'That is exactly what I do want you to do! Only make certain that Temple is in the basement before the water reaches the first grid.'

'Why, he'll be trapped like a rat!' gasped Guest.

But Ben was beginning to fall in with the idea.

'The idea is all right,' he said suddenly, 'if we can once get Temple into the basement.'

'You'll get him there,' pronounced Mrs Moffat calmly, 'if you use your head.'

Ben nodded thoughtfully. The more he thought of the idea, the better he liked it. After all, the loch was supposed to be deep, and there would certainly be no trace of the body.

'We'd better start packing the screen apparatus,' said van Draper suddenly. He was halfway to the door with Guest when Ben stopped him.

'Just a minute,' said Ben. 'What the devil happens to me after it's all over?'

'You'll meet Iris at the junction near High Moorford,' Mrs Moffat informed him. 'She'll bring you down to the chalet. Is that clear, Iris?'

The actress nodded, stubbed out her cigarette and rose.

'It looks as if I won't get that part in Temple's new play after all,' she murmured with just a trace of regret in her voice.

Ben turned to Guest.

'You'd better give me a hand with that pump. It takes a devil of a time to get it going,' he declared.

'All right,' said Guest.

'I'm off now,' decided Iris. 'I'll see you later, Ben.'

'OK,' he grunted, 'and for God's sake mind you're there in time.'

'I don't think Hardwick will give you any trouble,' said Mrs Moffat, 'but if he does, you'll know what to do.'

'Don't worry about Hardwick,' snapped van Draper. 'We'll handle him all right.'

'I can't see why the devil we should take Hardwick down to the chalet – just because of Temple,' Guest protested rather irritably. 'If we intend to get Temple, then why on earth don't we—'

Mrs Moffat silenced him with a gesture.

'We can't take any chances,' she told them. 'Not where Paul Temple is concerned.'

'H'm, perhaps you're right,' Guest conceded.

'Shall you come down to the chalet, Mrs Moffat?' asked Iris.

'No – at least, not till later.'

In answer to Iris' inquiring glance, she forced a smile. 'I can't – because of Z.4,' she said. 'I may be wanted.'

3

Paul Temple was not a little surprised to find the rather ornate gate to the drive of Skerry Lodge wide open. According to Bryant, Hubert C. Hardwick had found this very gate heavily padlocked. Could Bryant have been telling the truth? He made no comment to Steve. Whoever was at home in Skerry Lodge, reflected Temple, could not fail to hear the car approach. Soon the front porch came into full view, with a corner of Loch Abaford visible beyond a terrace to the right of the house. Temple drove boldly up to the rather massive front door and the car drew up with a slight screech of brakes.

He switched off the engine, and they sat in the car for two minutes surveying the landscape. After a little while Temple leapt out, and Steve joined him.

'By Timothy, Bryant was certainly right about this place,' Temple decided, looking up at the gaunt walls.

'Darling, don't you think we ought to go round to the side of the house before we try the front?' murmured Steve rather nervously.

'Sh!' said Temple, who was inside the front porch by now. 'There's someone coming.' He had rung the bell without Steve noticing it. 'Now it's perfectly all right, Steve. Don't get frightened.'

Heavy footsteps echoed on the stone flags inside, and presently the door was opened by Ben, who stood stiffly in the doorway.

'Good evening, sir.'

'Good evening,' replied Temple pleasantly. 'I should like to see Mr Hardwick. My name is—'

'Mr Hardwick is very busy just at the moment, sir, but if you'll step this way . . .'

'Thank you,' replied Temple. 'Come along, darling.'

Ben was rather taken aback to find Temple accompanied by his wife, but managed to conceal his surprise. He ushered them into the drawing room.

'What name shall I say, sir?'

'Temple – Paul Temple.'

'Thank you, sir,' said Ben gravely, and retired, closing the door firmly behind him.

Steve clutched her husband's arm.

'Paul,' she said in low urgent tones, tinged with alarm, 'Paul, we shouldn't have come here.'

'It's all right, darling,' repeated Temple reassuringly. He was busy taking rapid stock of his surroundings, and trying to work out a rough geography of the place. 'I say, it's a pretty decent sort of house, this. . . Certainly believes in doing himself well. . .' He crossed to the sideboard and thoughtfully surveyed the three empty whisky bottles and the large pile of cigarette ends on the ashtrays. 'There's been quite a party,' he mused.

Steve's voice brought him out of his reverie.

'I didn't notice Sir Graham when we left the inn,' she was saying. 'I hope you told him that we were coming here.'

'Sir Graham was telephoning – rather important, I should imagine.' Temple paced up and down the room. 'Hardwick must be worth a packet by the look of things,' he said. 'Just take a look at this picture!' He moved over to examine the oil painting rather more closely, then stopped short.

'What is it?' asked Steve.

'He's coming back.'

A moment later the bulky form of Ben loomed in the doorway.

'Mr Hardwick is extremely busy, sir,' he announced, 'but if you'd care to step down to his laboratory, I think he might be able to spare you a few moments.'

'Yes, of course,' Temple agreed. 'Come along, Steve.'

'I should leave your things here, sir,' interposed Ben, taking Temple's hat. 'You'll be able to pick them up on the way back.' He appropriated the light coat Steve was carrying and led the way along a short passage and down a flight of rather badly lighted stairs.

Directly facing them was a massive oak door, which Ben immediately flung open.

'This way, sir . . . this way, madam . . . Mr Hardwick will be along directly.'

The door closed, and Temple and Steve found themselves in a most unprepossessing cellar, lighted very dimly by partly concealed ventilators. An old table stood in the far corner of the room.

'Paul – I don't like the look of this place,' said Steve with a slight shiver.

'No, I'm not exactly enamoured myself,' Temple agreed.

Suddenly he walked swiftly to the door, turned the knob and pulled hard, but it seemed almost as immovable as the wall itself.

'Paul ... what is it?' cried Steve, noticing his jaw drop.

He was silent for a moment, making a last attempt to move the door.

'My God, Steve, we ought to have had more sense!' he murmured bitterly. 'We certainly shan't get out of here in a hurry!'

'But—why have they done this?' cried Steve. 'I can't understand—'

'For precisely the same reason that they left the car on "Hell's Elbow",' replied Temple grimly. 'Obviously, our visit wasn't the surprise I thought it would be.'

He brooded upon the situation for some minutes.

'Couldn't we break the door down?' suggested Steve at length, but Temple shook his head.

'Not this door, I'm afraid,' he said.

'Why is it padded at the foot?' asked Steve.

He bent down and examined the strip of heavy padding which had somehow been fastened on the underside of the door. Meanwhile Steve wandered away to take stock of the rest of the room. Underneath one of the ventilators she paused, listened, then looked upwards.

Her scream startled Temple in his contemplation of the door.

'Paul—look!'

He ran across to her and followed the indication of her trembling finger.

A thin stream of water was trickling steadily through the ventilator.

Temple caught his breath, then turned abruptly and ran across to the other ventilator. There was an even stronger stream flowing through it.

'My God!' he ejaculated. 'So that's what it is.'

'They're—they're flooding the room!' cried Steve.

They could hear the water quite distinctly now, as it tumbled through the ventilators in almost a miniature cascade.

Temple rushed across and shook the doorknob vigorously. The water was now about an inch deep on the floor.

'Open this door!' shouted Temple desperately, hammering at the panel with both fists.

'Paul, we've got to get out somehow,' she said.

'It's no use, I'm afraid,' he replied, turning away from the door. 'We'll just have to wait.' He sank onto the table, where Steve was already perched, watching the water slowly rising.

He placed an arm around her.

'Frightened, dear?' he whispered.

'Yes, I am rather,' she confessed. He clasped her shoulder reassuringly, though he felt far from hopeful.

For a second or two he gazed thoughtfully down at the water.

'At this rate, I should say we've got about an hour,' he estimated. 'Possibly longer – it's difficult to tell.'

Steve shivered.

'Cold, darling?'

She nodded without speaking and they were both silent for some minutes.

'Steve,' said Temple at length.

'Yes, darling?'

'I'm—I'm terribly sorry about this business.'

'Don't be silly, Paul.' She tried to smile bravely. 'It. . . it just can't be helped . . . that's all.'

Once again there was a long pause.

'There's nothing we can do, I'm afraid, except wait.'

'I suppose this room is on the side of the lake,' Steve speculated.

'Yes,' murmured Temple thoughtfully. 'It must be.' He took Steve's hand in his. 'It's funny, you know, I've often wondered how people reacted under circumstances like this; it's all so very unreal, and yet—' He hesitated. 'What is it, dear?'

'Nothing,' said Steve. 'I was just thinking – that's all.' There was a suspicious catch in her voice.

'Thinking?' repeated Temple, rather puzzled.

'Do you remember that first summer, darling?'

'Capri?'

'Yes – Capri. The blue sky . . . the gay little houses . . . the crazy little steamer . . . and the donkey.'

'Ah yes, the donkey,' Temple smiled reminiscently. 'A stubborn fellow at the best of times.'

He squeezed her hand. 'I'm sorry I landed you in this mess, darling.'

'It's . . . nothing,' said Steve, but there was a catch in her voice.

Suddenly Temple jumped off the table and crossed over to the door. He was both annoyed and irritated.

'Good God!' he cried in angry tones. 'We're talking as if the whole business were over and we were finished! We got ourselves into this, and we're going to get out of it.'

'It's no use, Paul,' said Steve, watching him throw his weight against the door.

But Temple still persisted. After awhile he rejoined her.

'I'm afraid the door is hopeless,' he declared gloomily. Then brightened a little. 'We might be able to stop the water, though.' He took off his coat, folded it into the smallest possible compass, and taking a chair, managed to wedge the garment into one of the ventilator grids. This reduced the flow considerably, but the water continued to rush through the other grid at an alarming rate.

'We shall hold out a little longer, at any rate,' he said.

Steve took off the coat of the costume she was wearing, and was about to follow her husband's example when she suddenly paused.

'Paul!' she cried suddenly.

'What is it?'

'Didn't you hear anything?'

'No,' he replied rather diffidently; he was concentrating on the flow of water. 'I don't think that coat of yours—'

'Paul—listen!'

They stood silent for a minute.

At first they could hear only the steady gush of water, then very faintly, almost like a distant echo, came the muffled voice of Sir Graham Forbes.

'Temple! Where are you, Temple?'

Desperately, Paul Temple turned towards the door.

'My God! It's Forbes! We've got to make him hear us, Steve.' For all they knew, Sir Graham might be at the other end of the house, and the water was rising rapidly.

'We'll have to be quick, darling!'

As Temple paused to regain his breath, he noticed that above the door was an old-fashioned fanlight, heavily smeared with dust and paint. It was so dirty as to be almost indistinguishable. Without another moment's hesitation, Temple seized a chair, and there was the sudden shattering of thick glass.

'Darling, you've cut yourself!' cried Steve in alarm.

'No, I'm all right,' he answered.

'Where the devil are you, Temple?' It was Forbes shouting and the voice sounded much nearer.

'We're at the end of the corridor,' cried Temple. 'For God's sake, be quick!'

There was a sound of footsteps running along the stone passage, and Steve gave a sigh of relief.

'Stand away from the door!' shouted Forbes.

'Stand back, Steve!' said Temple, taking her arm.

Several heavy blows fell on the door, and finally the panel splintered. Through the aperture they could see Forbes swinging a huge coal hammer and dealing heavy blows on the lock. As the lock gave way there was a rush of water which nearly swept the Chief Commissioner off his feet. The three of them managed to stagger up the stairs and out into the entrance hall.

'What's been going on here?' demanded Forbes, shaking himself.

'We'll explain later,' said Temple excitedly. 'Did you get any of them?'

'Yes,' replied Forbes, 'we arrested Ben and Iris Archer.'

'Iris?'

'Yes, she was in a car at the High Moorford junction – obviously waiting to pick him up.'

'Come on, Sir Graham – let's get back,' said Temple urgently.

A few moments later several Highland shepherds were more than a little mystified to see a hatless young man in shirt sleeves driving a car across the moors in a manner that completely ignored the existence of speed limits.

4

Iris Archer was making a bold attempt to conceal her annoyance. It had been irritating enough to be confined in the single cell of the local police station for a couple of hours with Ben as a companion, but she preferred even that to her present prospect of facing a battery of questions from Temple and Forbes. They were in Temple's room at the 'Royal Gate', a room with which Iris was by now quite familiar.

'Really, I can't for the life of me think what this is all about,' she said crossly, by way of opening the conversation.

'Sit down, Iris,' said Temple quietly, and, catching his level glance, she subsided. But, unlike Ben, Iris was quite calm.

'You've got nothing on me!' Ben shouted. 'I don't know anything – about anything.'

'You sound very helpful, I must say,' retorted Forbes grimly.

Paul Temple smiled.

'Where have they taken Hardwick?' he said.

'I don't know!' Suddenly Ben lost his temper. 'I don't know what the 'ell all this is about!'

'You soon will, my friend,' said Temple imperturbably.

'Where have they taken Hardwick?' Forbes repeated the question in rather a more businesslike tone.

'For God's sake don't keep on asking me the same ruddy questions!' cried Ben almost hysterically. He was about to continue, but the door opened quietly, and he hesitated.

Dr Ludwig Steiner stood in the doorway.

Instinctively all eyes turned towards the newcomer. Temple watched Ben and Iris very carefully, but they betrayed no sign of recognition.

'I am given to understand that you want to see me, Mr Temple,' said Steiner slowly.

'Yes, of course. Come in, Doctor.'

Then for the first time they saw that Rex Bryant was behind the Doctor's ample figure.

'Ah! Come in, Rex,' Temple invited.

'I hope I'm not intruding,' said Bryant with rather unusual politeness. 'But Steve said that you wanted a word with me.'

Forbes took the doctor's arm and led him over to where Iris was sitting.

'Doctor Steiner, is this the young lady who was with Mr Temple when—'

'Why, yes!' cried Steiner quickly. 'But of course—'

Iris looked at him impudently, then with a slight shrug turned away.

'Have you seen this man before, Doctor?' continued Forbes, indicating Ben.

Steiner wrinkled his brow. 'Why, no – not that I am aware of,' he said.

'What about you, Bryant?' queried Forbes, turning to Rex.

Rex paused a moment before answering. 'No, I haven't seen him before.'

'You've seen Iris Archer before, naturally?' Forbes persisted.

Rex grinned. 'I was once a dramatic critic for one night,' he recalled. 'And I'm afraid Miss Archer was one of my—er—victims. I should like to take this opportunity of apologising.'

He gave a polite bow, but Iris completely ignored him.

'Mr Richmond, you must forgive me,' Steiner interposed, 'but I am afraid I do not understand—'

'My name is not Richmond, sir,' said Forbes brusquely. 'It's Forbes – Sir Graham Forbes of Scotland Yard.'

'Scotland Yard,' repeated Steiner thoughtfully, rolling the consonants with undue emphasis. 'That explains a great deal.'

'It doesn't explain what the 'ell I'm doing here,' Ben snarled.

'I think you have a pretty good idea about that,' said Temple, regarding him intently.

'Look here, Paul, this is getting beyond a joke—' Iris was beginning to protest, when Temple interrupted her in a tone that was unduly ruthless for him.

'I'm inclined to agree, Iris – it *is* beyond a joke. A man was killed yesterday near Skellyfore.'

'I don't know what on earth you're talking about,' she replied coldly.

The door opened rather suddenly to reveal Mrs Weston. She was holding a telegram.

'I'll take it, Mrs Weston,' said Sir Graham.

'It's addressed to someone called Forbes,' she pointed, out. 'I told the boy we hadn't anybody of that name staying 'ere, but the cheeky young monkey wouldn't wait.'

'That's all right, Mrs Weston,' nodded Forbes quickly, and almost closed the door himself. There was a silence while Forbes rapidly tore open the flimsy envelope. After he had read the message he looked up. His gaze was directed at Ben.

'Your name is Collins,' he said slowly. 'Roy Benjamin Collins. You are wanted for the murder of a girl named Rita Allenby.'

'It's a lie!' shouted Ben. 'You can't pin a "rap" on me like that.' He looked round wildly at the door and window, as if searching for a means of escape.

'We don't have to pin anything, Ben,' said Forbes calmly. 'The facts are here.' He indicated the slip of orange paper.

Once more Ben looked round like a trapped animal.

'What is it you want to know?'

'Where have they taken Hardwick?' asked Forbes quietly.

'I don't know,' muttered Ben. 'For God's sake, leave me alone!'

'Ben, if you pull yourself together, I might be inclined to overlook this afternoon's incident,' said Temple.

'Don't you see, you've got to tell us the truth sooner or later?' Forbes rapped out.

'But I've told you,' protested Ben, 'I don't know anything.'

'How did you know that Temple was leaving for Aberdeen in the morning?' said Forbes.

Suddenly Ben made up his mind to talk. If Scotland Yard already knew about Rita Allenby, he reflected, then obviously he had nothing to lose.

'Mrs Moffat told us,' he replied. 'She came to the house—'

'Mrs Moffat!' echoed Forbes, more than a little surprised.

Iris jumped up from her chair. 'Shut up!' she ordered desperately, addressing Ben for the first time. 'Keep your mouth shut, you damn' fool, or . . .'

Temple quietly interposed himself between Iris and Ben.

'Carry on, Ben. Mrs Moffat came to the house and—'

'She came to the house,' continued Ben, licking his lips nervously, 'and told us that she'd received instructions from—'

'Ben, for God's sake keep your mouth shut!' shrieked Iris.

'That she had received instructions from Z.4?' suggested Temple.

Ben nodded. 'Yes . . . from Z.4.'

'How did Mrs Moffat receive the instructions?'

'I—I don't remember.'

'Ben—' Temple reproved him gently.

'I don't remember, I tell you! Let me get out of here!'

Forbes waved the telegram form suggestively. 'We've got to know how Mrs Moffat received those instructions,' he said quietly.

'I don't know! I don't know!' cried Ben hysterically. He seemed to be almost on the verge of a nervous collapse, and Steiner regarded him with a certain amount of alarm.

'Sir Graham,' he suggested tentatively.

Forbes did not relish the interruption, but Steiner insisted. 'Perhaps a drink would enable him to—'

Ben looked up.

'Yes . . . get me a drink. Please get me a drink,' he begged.

Sir Graham nodded and turned towards the bell push.

'I'll slip downstairs,' Rex offered, but Temple forestalled him.

'There's no need for that, Rex. I've got a flask here.'

He took a small flask from his coat pocket and unscrewed the cap. The flask was new and probably held about half a pint.

'Scotch?' asked Ben, and Temple nodded.

It had just occurred to Forbes that it was rather unusual for the novelist to carry a flask, when his gaze rested on Ben.

Ben had already taken a very long drink, and there was something both strange and rather frightening about the way he was staring. The flask dangled from his fingers and after a second or two fell with a clatter onto the wooden floor. Suddenly his head fell forward too, as if he was still anxious to keep his eyes on the flask without the necessary effort of moving his body.

Sir Graham was puzzled. He made a movement towards Ben, but a sudden exclamation from Iris made him halt.

'My God!' cried Iris. 'He's dead!'

Forbes crossed over to Ben and took hold of his wrist. After a little while he looked up.

'Yes, he's dead all right,' he said quietly.

'Then I think perhaps under the circumstances you had better take care of this, Sir Graham,' said Temple, and picked up the flask.

'My God, Temple!' breathed Iris, in complete bewilderment. 'You killed him – you killed him!'

Temple shook his head. He seemed completely unshaken by the sudden turn of events.

'I didn't kill him, Iris,' he said quietly. 'Ben was killed by Z.4.'

'Z.4!' cried Iris, and there was no mistaking the astonishment in her voice.

It must be recorded that for some unknown reason Rex Bryant was looking at Doctor Steiner.

CHAPTER V

In Which Mrs Moffat Receives a Visitor

1

John Hardwick was an embittered man. His rather simple outlook on life, which was a natural outcome of his calling, had been badly bruised in the course of its contacts with the War Office.

After expending far more nervous energy than he could afford in threading his way through the annoying departmental inquiries and counter-inquiries, his patience was at an end. When he had at last discovered an official capable of comprehending his technical language, he managed to arrange various tests for the Hardwick Screen.

By a stroke of ill-luck, a trifling hitch had upset the final tests, and rather than offer him a little human encouragement the officials had put in a half-hearted report that was now gathering dust in the files.

After several weeks of irksome inquiries Hardwick had received the shabby specification in a registered envelope.

About two months after his visit to the War Office Hardwick received a visitor in the person of Major Guest. Guest drew a very pleasant picture of a perfectly equipped laboratory in the wilds of Scotland, where no outsider would interfere, and where there was every facility for experiment.

Reasonably enough, he pointed out that no inventor immersed in his job could be expected to market his inventions to the best advantage. No one saw his point more clearly than Hardwick. It seemed that Guest represented a syndicate which could be relied upon to negotiate the screen with a more interested party than the War Office. All they asked in return was a third share of the proceeds. Since they had to fit up a laboratory in a large house which they had already purchased at considerable expense, in addition to making all the arrangements for the disposal of the screen, this seemed fair enough.

Hardwick had by this time remedied the flaw in the Hardwick Screen, and was eager to start work on the Hardwick Beam, which would involve the purchase of several crates of costly apparatus. To say the least, this offer was opportune.

In any case, John Hardwick was never particularly interested in money, except as a medium for the acquiring of the apparatus he needed. All he asked from life was a simple mode of existence and eighteen hours a day to devote to his experiments.

He was basically a dreamer, but recent events had developed a certain shrewdness in his make-up. Outside his own work he closed up like an oyster.

At Skerry Lodge he took no particular notice of the people who received him. They saw that his bodily comforts were attended to, and procured any particular piece of apparatus he wanted at exceptionally short notice. He was, in fact, left very much to himself, and all that was asked of him was a weekly report detailing progress to date and written as simply as possible. This was read by Guest and van Draper, then forwarded to Z.4 under various fictitious names at *post restantes*.

On his arrival, Hardwick had been asked for the specifications of the screen, but it was understood that these were to be kept in the safe at Skerry Lodge, and should be available to either party. As his hosts politely pointed out, they might have to produce evidence that they had the goods to deliver.

Hardwick was not particularly interested in the nationality of any such purchaser. Any traces of patriotism in his make-up had been very firmly erased during his negotiations with the War Office. Of course, if Great Britain made the best bid they were welcome to the Hardwick Screen. The inventor was quite indifferent.

This attitude could not have suited Guest and van Draper better. Hardwick gave them very little trouble; in fact he might almost have been one of the organisation. All the same, they had a shrewd suspicion that once the beam was perfected, Z.4 would not be content with a third share.

A few weeks after his arrival, Hardwick had suggested that they might like a demonstration of the screen, and this had proved so successful that Guest, who was well informed on military matters, had sent a special report to Z.4, urging an immediate disposal of the screen. But Z.4 had preferred to await the result of the beam experiments, which would more than double the value of the first invention.

His experiences with the War Office had bred a certain amount of caution in Hardwick. Although his reports appeared quite comprehensive, they did not contain every detail. In fact, he was keeping back just enough detail to prevent any appropriation of his ideas until he received his share of the proceeds. Somehow, he did not altogether trust

Guest and van Draper. He didn't quite know why, though for that matter he hardly trusted anyone nowadays except his brother Hubert. Strange he had not heard from Hubert for some time. He usually wrote about once a week. A short flippant letter telling of some recent misadventure. He had written twice to Hubert without receiving a reply, which rather worried him.

Hardwick had been so absorbed in his work that he had not noticed the atmosphere of strain that had become very apparent at Skerry Lodge during the past week. Guest and van Draper had been careful to conceal it as much as possible on the few occasions they were in contact with Hardwick. So the inventor was more than a little startled when van Draper entered his laboratory one day and peremptorily ordered him to pack up as much apparatus as he could, leaving nothing of any importance.

Hardwick was inclined to resent this. He ran his hands through his thinning hair in some perplexity and frowned. Van Draper was impatient.

'There's no time to be lost!' he snapped.

The inventor still appeared bewildered.

'We've got to get out of here – half of Scotland Yard will soon be on the doorstep,' rasped van Draper.

'But look here—' Hardwick began to protest.

Van Draper made an impatient gesture. 'If you don't pack up and come along now, this will mean the end of all your experiments, and our chance to sell the screen.'

But Hardwick was still perplexed.

'I still don't see what right anyone has to interfere—' he was beginning, when van Draper cut him short.

'It seems as if I'll have to use a little persuasion,' he declared. And Hardwick found himself looking into the barrel of the neat little revolver.

John Hardwick shrugged his shoulders helplessly, and turned to pack his apparatus.

2

Even the placid Steiner was plainly upset by the revolting spectacle of Ben's death agonies. It appeared as if Temple had engineered the whole business, and Temple had always seemed such a trustworthy sort of person. Why should he wish to be rid of Ben, who seemed to be on the verge of divulging some rather important evidence? And now he declared that Z.4 was the man who had been responsible for the murder.

'Z.4? But I do not understand. Who is this Z.4, and what—' he was beginning, when Rex Bryant interrupted.

'What's in that flask, Sir Graham?' he demanded abruptly.

Forbes sniffed the flask rather tentatively. He paused, then sniffed again. At last he spoke.

'Cyanide,' he murmured softly.

'Cyanide!' echoed Rex with a shudder. 'No wonder the poor devil went through hell.' He regarded the body with a puzzled frown.

Steiner was equally perplexed.

'But surely you must have known, Mr Temple,' he gasped incredulously.

'Of course he knew,' snapped Iris angrily, but Temple ignored her and faced Steiner.

'Doctor, do you really think I'd have given him that flask if I'd had any idea of the contents?'

Steiner shook his head helplessly.

'No—no—of course not,' he replied with an expressive gesture. 'Naturally, I would not dream of suggesting—' He broke off in obvious dismay.

'That's all right, Doctor,' Temple cut in quietly.

But Iris was not to be denied. Hands on hips, she stared at Temple accusingly.

'It seems quite obvious to me,' she pronounced deliberately. 'If Z.4 killed Ben – then Paul Temple is Z.4.'

There was a dry chuckle from Sir Graham, but the others were silent. Temple was the first to speak.

'It's an interesting theory, Iris,' he smiled. 'An interesting theory, if nothing else.'

'I agree, Temple,' said Forbes. 'Maybe it wouldn't stand up to close examination – still, it's a theory.'

'There's no need to be so damned smug about it,' cried Iris angrily. 'We know that Temple gave Ben the flask, and we know from what Mrs Moffat said that Z.4 is here at the inn—'

Realising that she had said too much, she stopped short.

'What did Mrs Moffat say?' Temple asked quietly.

There was a pause. Iris looked at each of them in turn. Steiner was obviously awaiting her reply with some eagerness; so was Sir Graham. Rex was bending over Ben, and apparently taking little notice of the conversation. Temple's face was quite expressionless, but his rather dreamy eyes had taken on a piercing quality.

'You were about to tell us what Mrs Moffat said,' he reminded her politely.

'Nothing,' retorted Iris with an air of bravado. 'Nothing at all.'

'Then,' proceeded Temple, 'perhaps you wouldn't mind explaining that remark of yours.'

Iris appeared to flare up again.

'If there's any explaining to be done, don't you think you ought to explain away this murder? Where did you get that flask?'

'Yes,' put in Forbes, falling into Iris' trap to sidetrack the conversation, 'where did you get that flask?'

Temple smiled rather sleepily.

'Well, it's a long story,' he began. 'An uncle of mine who keeps an antique shop in Bangkok has a passion for these flasks . . . Chinese flasks, Japanese flasks, Russian flasks. It's positively astounding . . .'

With annoying deliberation he paused and lit a cigarette.

'Though I suppose it isn't astounding really,' he went on. 'Because, you see, he isn't really my uncle . . . after all.'

There was a quiet laugh from Rex, who seemed to be the only one to appreciate that Temple was playing Iris at her own game.

'Well . . . er . . . I think we'll leave the question of the flask for the time being,' said Forbes at length. He realised that Temple had some reason for not wishing Iris to know the story of the flask.

'Why should we leave it?' demanded Iris. 'Just because—'

'Just because there's a more important question, Iris,' Temple quietly informed her.

'A more important question?'

Temple threw his cigarette into the grate.

'Where have they taken John Hardwick?' he demanded abruptly.

If Iris was surprised to hear the name she did not show it.

'I don't know what you are talking about,' she answered.

'Don't you, Iris? Perhaps Mrs Moffat would enlighten you.'

'Mrs Moffat? Who is this Mrs Moffat?' asked Steiner, still very mystified.

'I say!' cried Rex, suddenly enlightened. 'You don't mean the old girl in the village with the elastic-sided boots? The old dear in the sweet shop-cum-post office?'

Temple nodded.

'Well, how on earth does she fit into all this?' Rex was anxious to discover.

'You know Mrs Moffat?' demanded Forbes, eyeing him intently.

'Well, I don't exactly *know* her,' replied Rex. 'I've been in the shop once or twice, that's all.' He seemed to be about to enlarge on this, but Sir Graham cut him short. He exchanged a glance with Temple, then turned towards Rex once more.

'I should consider it a favour, Bryant, if you and Dr Steiner would leave us for a short while.'

'Yes, yes!' Steiner readily agreed. 'We are in the way, young man. Come along!'

Rex followed him lazily to the door.

'There's nothing like a subtle hint, is there, Temple?' he grinned. 'I presume this is one of the many occasions when the police consider it is not advisable for the Press to be represented. Come along, Doctor, you can buy me a large glass of your favourite lager.'

When the door had closed, Forbes and Temple returned to Iris once more.

'Now, Iris—' began Temple quietly.

'What's this a cue for?' she demanded insolently, standing with her back to the fireplace and eyeing them with a certain amount of contempt. The pose suited her admirably, and even Sir Graham could not help reflecting that her beauty was more than a little startling in spite of her recent experiences. But Temple was quite unimpressed.

'We want to know where they have taken John Hardwick,' he declared flatly.

'And who, precisely, are "they"?' she replied, a contemptuous smile flickering around the finely chiselled lips.

But Temple had decided that they had no more time to waste.

'Listen, Iris,' he said in determined tones, 'there's been quite enough beating about the bush . . .'

'All right,' she agreed, 'let's stop beating about it.' But she made no attempt to answer the question. After a while the Chief Commissioner spoke.

'Miss Archer, I don't know whether you realise it or not, but I have a warrant for your arrest.'

'On what charge?'

'Attempted murder.'

Iris was obviously taken by surprise.

'The cigarette, Iris,' Temple reminded her softly. 'Remember the cigarette?'

A thoughtful expression passed swiftly across her features, then she laughed lightly.

'You'll never get away with that, Temple. Why, how can you prove that—'

'You seem to have overlooked the fact that I have a witness,' said Temple. 'Doctor Steiner came into the room and caught you.'

'And who the hell is Dr Steiner?' cried Iris angrily. 'It's only a case of his word against mine.'

'It needn't be a case of anything, Iris,' Temple interposed suavely, 'if you use your head.'

'What do you mean?'

'I just want you to answer a question.'

'Well?'

'Are you Z.4?'

Iris straightened herself sharply.

'No!' she cried almost desperately.

'Then,' persisted Temple, 'who is?'

She shook her head. 'I don't know.'

'Mrs Moffat?' suggested Temple sofdy.

'I don't know, I tell you,' she replied petulantly.

'All right,' Temple nodded. 'A little while ago you said
"We know from what Mrs Moffat said that Z.4 is here at
the inn". ... How do we know that Z.4 is here?'

Iris hesitated, but replied eventually: 'Because Mrs Moffat
received a message from Z.4.'

'Was the message received the night before Steve and I
left for Aberdeen?'

'Yes.'

'My God, Temple!' cried Sir Graham, striding swiftly up
and down, 'it seems to prove that Mrs Moffat is right. Only
someone staying at the inn could possibly have known that
you and Steve were leaving.'

But Temple was concentrating on Iris.

'If Mrs Moffat isn't Z.4, does she know who Z.4 really
is?' he continued.

'No,' answered Iris; 'not yet.'

Temple nodded slowly as he turned over the significance
of the last remark.

'But surely Guest or van Draper must have made contact,'
interrupted Forbes rather excitedly.

Iris smiled enigmatically – a smile that had gone a long
way to making her famous.

'No one knows the identity of Z.4, Sir Graham,' she told
him. 'Not even the infallible Paul Temple.'

But Temple refused to rise to the bait. All he said was: 'I
shouldn't be too sure of that, Iris, if I were you.'

There was something in his voice which made both
Iris and Forbes pause. Their reflections were interrupted,
however, by a knock at the door. Forbes looked apprehen-
sively at the body.

'That sounds like Mrs Weston,' he said. 'We'd better keep her out of here.'

'It's all right – she can't see Ben from the door,' Temple reassured him. When he opened the door, Mrs Weston was waiting with a telegram.

'Just arrived, Mr Temple – it's for you this time.'

Temple took the envelope, which was somewhat crumpled.

'Looks as if it's been opened,' she murmured.

Temple was scanning the message.

'All right, thanks, Mrs Weston. No reply.' He closed the door.

'Anything important?' asked Forbes.

Temple shook his head. He thrust the envelope into his pocket and resumed the cross-examination.

'Iris, what do you mean by saying that Mrs Moffat doesn't know who Z.4 is—*yet*? What does that "yet" imply?'

She shrugged her shoulders. 'It can imply just what the devil you like.'

Temple took a step nearer. 'You've got to tell us more about Mrs Moffat,' he said grimly.

'And you've also got to tell us where they've taken Hardwick,' added Forbes.

'I don't know where they've taken Hardwick. I've told you that already,' she replied coolly.

'And Mrs Moffat?'

Iris seemed disconcerted for a moment. Then she said steadily: 'There's nothing more to tell about Mrs Moffat. And if you think I'm going to spend the rest of the night going through a blasted third degree, then you're very much mistaken.'

'Very well, Miss Archer,' said Forbes smoothly. 'If you have no wish to answer any further questions, that's quite in order.'

His manner made Iris apprehensive.

'What's going to happen now?' she was anxious to know.

'You'll spend the night here,' Forbes informed her coldly. 'Tomorrow, Detective Inspector Fuller will take you to Glasgow.'

'Under arrest?'

'Of course.'

Temple made one last attempt.

'Iris, don't be a fool!' he urged. 'You know perfectly well what they've done with Hardwick.'

'Oh, for God's sake leave me alone!' she said in a voice that was very near to tears.

Temple said: 'I'm sorry, Iris, but we've got to find out what they've done to John Hardwick!'

'I don't know!' she cried. 'How many more times do I have to tell you?'

'It's no use, Temple,' growled Forbes.

There was silence for a few moments. Though she had momentarily allowed her emotions to get the better of her, Iris made a quick recovery. Eventually she spoke quite calmly: 'Since I have apparently no other alternative but to spend the night here, perhaps you will be good enough to show me to my room,' she suggested.

'Yes – all right,' Forbes agreed.

He was moving over to the door when Temple stopped him.

'Wait a moment,' said the novelist.

'What is it?' demanded Iris, in tones of exaggerated weariness.

Temple took the orange envelope from his pocket.

'I'd like you to know the contents of this telegram, Iris.'

'It can't possibly interest me,' she protested, though there was an element of doubt in her voice.

'That,' said Temple slowly, 'is a matter of opinion.'

'What does it say, Temple?' asked Forbes.

'It was handed in at Nice at five-thirty this evening,' continued Temple. 'Perhaps you'd like to read it for yourself.'

He passed the flimsy paper over to Iris. She read:

Thanks for telegram. Information you require as follows:
Hotel Martinez. April fourteenth nineteen thirty-two.

The telegram fell from Iris' fingers.

'Look out, Temple, she's going to faint!' cried Forbes.

But Temple had anticipated this. Carefully he lowered Iris into an armchair.

'She's passed out all right,' commented Forbes drily, picking up the telegram.

'Hotel Martinez . . . April the fourteenth, nineteen thirty-two . . .' he repeated.

The Chief Commissioner looked across at Paul Temple. He was obviously bewildered.

3

The first-class waiting room at High Moorford Junction is one of the last places on earth in which one would choose to wait. In fact, most passengers preferred to linger on the platform, except in very cold weather, when there was a faint glimmer of fire in the rusty grate.

The dirty green walls had been recklessly scribbled upon, and even the generously coloured posters depicting the alluring attractions of the Sunny South had a dowdy appearance. Though the waiting room was swept out daily, one could feel the dust hanging in the atmosphere, and it came as no surprise to see cobwebs in distant corners.

It was towards midday when Detective Inspector Fuller and Iris Archer entered the waiting room, followed by Andy Claike, whose stationmaster's uniform looked as if it would be the better for the vigorous application of a clothes brush.

Fuller was not in the best of tempers, for he had been misinformed about the train services. And Andy Claike had not been exactly helpful, beyond shaking his head mournfully and insisting that they would have to change for Glasgow.

'And how long have we got to wait here?' Fuller was saying as they entered the waiting room.

'Ye can't tell,' replied Andy with an indifferent shrug.

'Not long, I hope,' put in Iris.

'Ye can't tell,' repeated Andy woodenly.

'They told us at Inverdale that it was a through train,' Fuller insisted.

'Och, they must have forgotten the trains have been altered for the autumn schedule,' Andy suggested.

'I see – then it's a good job you yanked us out in time,' said Fuller.

'Do you think I might have a cigarette, Inspector?' asked Iris. 'Or would that be asking too much?'

Fuller shook his head. 'I'm sorry, miss. That would be against my instructions.' He turned to Andy once more. 'Look here – are you quite certain that we change here for Glasgow?'

'I'm stationmaster here,' replied Andy with sudden dignity.

'I didn't ask you that!' Fuller snapped.

'Ye'll be here three hours at least,' Claike calmly informed him. 'The next train is at three-fifteen.'

'Three-fifteen!' echoed Fuller in astonishment.

Andy nodded. 'That's what I said.'

'But, good heavens, man,' snorted Fuller in exasperation, 'we can't stay in here all that time!'

If Andy resented this criticism of the waiting room, he showed no sign of it.

'There's always the platform, of course,' he replied indifferently.

'Look here,' went on Fuller in some desperation, 'my name's Fuller – Detective Inspector Fuller.'

'How d'ye do?' muttered Andy, quite unimpressed. 'Andy Claike's the name – stationmaster.'

'Your sparkling personality doesn't seem to have registered, Inspector,' smiled Iris.

Fuller shook himself impatiently.

'Mr Claike, I don't think you quite appreciate the urgency of my business,' he rasped.

'The next train to Glasgow will be at three-fifteen,' Claike put in quietly. 'It would still be at three-fifteen, Mr Fuller, if you were the Czar of Russia.'

'But there isn't a Czar of Russia any longer, Mr Claike,' interposed Iris brightly. 'Hasn't the news reached here yet?' Andy regarded her curiously, then turned to Fuller.

'Who is this young woman?' he demanded quietly. 'I've seen her before somewhere—'

Fuller did not attempt to answer his question.

'Have you a telephone here?' he demanded.

'There's one in the office,' Andy informed him. 'It'll cost ye—'

'That's all right. Where's the office?'

'At the end of the platform – near the slot machine.'

Fuller turned to Iris. 'I'm going to telephone for a car. We can't stay here until three-fifteen – God knows when we'd get to Glasgow.'

'You think of everything, Inspector,' said Iris sarcastically. 'Anyhow, I'm not in any hurry.'

'Well, I am!' snapped Fuller. 'I've got a wife and kids waiting for me.'

Iris shrugged. 'It must take nerve to marry a policeman,' she said.

Fuller smiled and went across to Claike again.

'I want you to stay here while I telephone.'

'I have my job to be getting on with, ye know,' Andy pointed out.

Fuller ignored the remark.

'Is there a key to this door?'

Andy nodded.

'I should like it, please.'

'But look here—' the stationmaster began to protest, when Iris broke in with her rippling laugh.

'It's quite all right, Mr Claike. You see, I'm a desperate criminal, so naturally the Inspector must take all the necessary precautions.'

Andy gave a mirthless chuckle.

'Yes, well, I'm quite capable of lookin' after a wee lass – though I may not be a policeman.'

Fuller gave him a shrewd glance.

'H'm . . . all right,' he agreed at length. 'I shan't be long.'

The door closed with a squeak of protest, and the Inspector's heavy footsteps echoed along the platform.

A tank engine puffed breathlessly in one of the sidings. A goods train clanked its way dismally through the station and the whistle of a distant express came shrilling over the moors. Iris took her cigarette case from her bag, then replaced it. Suddenly she went over to the stationmaster, took off his hat, and broke into waves of hysterical laughter.

'My God! What a make-up! Darling, I could have screamed.' She replaced the hat. 'Where's Laurence?'

Guest adjusted his hat carefully. 'He's in the office – waiting for the Inspector.'

'Poor old Fuller – not a bad sort, if he didn't take his work so seriously. I'm afraid he's in for a warm reception.' She perched on the edge of the table. 'Tell me, how did it all happen?'

Guest smiled. 'Mrs Moffat must take the credit for the idea,' he admitted.

'Mrs Moffat?'

'Yes. She knew that the train stopped at High Moorford. Apparently this particular train always does.'

'But the stationmaster?'

Guest laughed. 'It didn't take us long to handle poor old Claike, although young Merson was certainly a handful.'

'Merson?'

'He's the porter,' Guest explained. 'And how that boy can wallop.' He rubbed his jaw rather gingerly.

'But what have you done with these people?'

'Claike's all right. We dumped him in a goods wagon on the other side of the line. Merson, I regret to say, overstepped the bounds of discretion, so we had to put him to sleep rather forcibly.'

The door opened with its customary groan, and van Draper came in.

'She's all right then?' he asked, with a sharp glance at Iris.

Iris nodded. 'Yes, I'm all right.'

Van Draper was obviously ill at ease.

'We'd better get away from here, Guest, and damn' quickly, too,' he announced.

'What's happened?'

'It's Fuller.' Van Draper sighed. 'My God, that man was a handful.'

Guest took Iris by the arm. As they made for the door, he began issuing instructions.

'Your car's outside, Iris. Make straight for the chalet – you know the way. Straight through the village and bear left about a mile from Aberford.'

Iris halted.

'But what about you and Laurence?'

'We have to see Mrs Moffat. We'll join you at the chalet later.'

'I see.' Iris paused, then suddenly faced van Draper. 'Laurence, how did Mrs Moffat know that I should be on that particular train?'

'She received the information from Z.4,' replied van Draper coolly.

Iris' smooth brow contracted. She was more than a little puzzled.

'Z.4 hasn't contacted her yet. . . personally, I mean?'

Van Draper shook his head.

Iris still seemed very uneasy. She looked at each man in turn, but their faces were inscrutable.

'Then I'll see you both later. . . at the chalet?' she murmured at length.

'We shall be there about four,' assented van Draper quietly.

Iris was still patently uncomfortable, but neither man offered any further explanation. Finally, with a tiny shrug, she went to the door.

'I'll show you where your car is parked, Iris,' offered van Draper.

'Thanks.' She turned to Guest. 'See you later.'

Guest nodded. 'Goodbye, Iris.'

When they had gone, Guest strolled round the waiting room, whistling softly to himself. Through the grimy window he saw van Draper and Iris disappear down the station drive. He was just deciding to change out of his uniform, when the door was flung open and a calm voice said: 'Drop that gun!'

His movement forestalled, Guest dropped his revolver. Detective Inspector Fuller crossed over and picked it up.

'How . . . how the devil did you get out?' stammered Guest.

Fuller ignored the question.

'Where's the other man?' he demanded rapidly.

'I don't know who you're talking about,' stalled Guest, his brain working quickly.

'Where is he?' insisted Fuller. 'Where is the swine?'

Fuller was obviously desperate.

'I tell you I don't know,' replied Guest with some heat.

'By God, if there's any more funny business in this place—' began Fuller.

'Look out!' shouted Guest suddenly.

The door had creaked again. Fuller swung round, but he was too late. There was the sharp crack of a revolver and, clutching his left side, the detective crumpled into a heap.

Guest bent over the inert form, then straightened himself.

'Good job you shouted,' said van Draper quietly, 'otherwise I don't think I would have got him in time.'

'No – perhaps not,' agreed Guest softly. 'That shot must have echoed—'

'I doubt if it was heard above all that shunting that's going on.'

Guest nodded. 'All the same, we'd better get out of here, Van.' He went to the door, looked round cautiously, then beckoned to van Draper. Putting on a bold front, they walked out of the waiting room, along the platform and towards van Draper's car, which was parked just outside.

After they had proceeded for perhaps half a mile, Guest asked the question which had been uppermost in his mind since van Draper's return.

'Did Iris get—'

'Yes,' replied the other, rather impatiently. 'She got away all right. The car appeared quite normal.'

Guest wrinkled his brow, pursed his lips and nodded.

'How far do you think she'll get before anything happens?' asked van Draper, deftly changing gear.

'H'm, difficult to tell. Perhaps a couple of miles. The roads are pretty bad, you know, and she drives like the devil.'

'She'll certainly be stepping on it at the moment – good and hard. There isn't much fear of us overtaking her just yet.'

'Van, why do you think Mrs Moffat heard from Z.4 about Iris?' said Guest, who did not altogether like the look of things.

'It's all perfectly obvious,' said van Draper. 'Iris must have been on the verge of talking – that's why Z.4 worked out this pretty little plan.'

'And I had instructions to "doctor" the car?'

Van Draper nodded. 'I feel rather sorry about Iris,' he mused, frowning thoughtfully at the winding road ahead. 'She had great charm, if nothing else.'

'Yes,' agreed Guest slowly. 'Great charm . . .'

For some minutes each man was busy with his own thoughts. They swung round a corner, and began to overtake a blue saloon ahead.

'That car's familiar,' muttered Guest thoughtfully. Suddenly he clutched van Draper's arm. 'Don't pass them, Van!'

'Why not?'

'It's Temple – and his wife!'

Van Draper peered at the car in front.

'So it is.'

'Don't pass them,' repeated Guest. 'We don't want to run up against Temple just now.'

Van Draper nodded, and the car slowed down to a steady thirty miles an hour.

4

In spite of the fact that she was not feeling very much like a drive, Temple had persuaded Steve to go out with him. In the first place, he found that driving a car often helped him to solve little problems, and the constant change of scene frequently gave him new ideas. Also, he had some vague notion of keeping a sharp lookout for a likely hideout where Hardwick might be kept a prisoner. Finally, he decided that he must get away from the 'Royal Gate Inn', where even his very thoughts seemed to be divined by some mysterious means.

As they approached the village of Skellyfore, Temple felt the urgent need for a cigarette, only to find he had left his case in another coat.

'Got any cigarettes, Steve?' he asked. She opened her bag and produced an empty case. He laughed, and took his foot off the accelerator preparatory to slowing down.

'Shan't be a second,' he told her, jumping out and slamming the door. Then, rather to Steve's surprise, he reopened it and jumped into the car again. 'I'll move forward a bit. Not a very safe place to park at the foot of this hill,' he murmured. As he released the handbrake, Steve asked: 'What time did you arrange to meet Sir Graham?'

'I said about two. We're rather early, as a matter of fact.'

'What on earth made you suggest meeting at the café at High Moorford? Surely it would have been much easier to have waited at the inn?'

'No,' answered Temple quietly. 'I wanted to have a talk with Forbes away from the inn. I've got a funny sort of feeling about the "Royal Gate"...'

'What do you mean?'

'Everything that happens at the inn – every conversation that takes place there, seems by some means or other to be known to Z.4.'

Steve thought for a moment. 'Yes, that's true,' she conceded at length. 'They knew, for instance, that we were starting for Aberdeen and—'

She broke off sharply as she saw her husband's attention had wandered.

'Look at that car coming down the hill,' he said quickly. 'By Timothy, it's lurching all over the place!'

Steve followed his glance and saw a smart little sports car careering giddily from one side of the narrow road to the other. Fortunately there was very little traffic in this quiet village, but the car narrowly missed a baker's cart and appeared to be about to mount the kerb. Temple saw the girl driver wrench vigorously at the wheel, and the car slid back into the roadway to continue its crazy course.

'There must be something wrong with it, Paul,' cried Steve. 'The steering or—'

'Good God!' ejaculated Temple. 'Look – it's Iris!'

The car was less than fifty yards away from them now. Iris was plainly visible.

'She'll never get that car straight – she'll never do it, Steve!'

'But it can't be Iris,' Steve heard herself stammering incredulously. 'She couldn't have got away from the detective and—'

'There's something wrong with the steering!' gasped Temple. 'My God – she's going for the pavement!'

Iris suddenly abandoned her unequal struggle with the steering and flung her arms in front of her as the car leapt over the gutter and crashed into the window of a general store.

People appeared on the scene with magic celerity, and in less than two minutes well over half the population of the little village were clustered round the car. Steve had seen the figure in bright green flung violently forward at the moment of impact; then she had instinctively turned her head away.

Temple jumped out of the car.

'Wait here, Steve,' he ordered, and rushed off towards the wrecked car.

He managed to push his way through the group of onlookers, some of whom obviously mistook him for a doctor.

Iris was huddled in a corner of the front seat. Blood was trickling from a cut on her cheek, and her left arm hung limply over the steering wheel. Her eyes were half closed, but she was not unconscious. A man came rushing from a public house opposite and thrust a small glass of brandy into Temple's hand. Temple put the glass to her over-red lips and managed to force a few drops into her mouth. There was a smear of lipstick on the glass. Her eyelids fluttered the merest trifle.

'Are you all right, Iris?' he demanded urgently.

She ran her tongue over the red lips and blinked at him rather uncertainly.

'What are you doing here?' she gasped, and made as if to straighten herself. But the well-moulded features were suddenly distorted with a violent spasm of pain, and she relapsed into her former position.

'It's . . . all right,' she murmured shakily. 'It's only my shoulder . . . a bit of a sprain, I think . . .'

'By Timothy, you're lucky to be alive!' Temple told her.

'Something went wrong with the steering,' she muttered in bewildered tones. 'I could feel it as soon as—' Her voice drifted into an incoherent murmur. Suddenly her eyes opened fully and her features tightened. 'The swine! The damned swine!' She spat out the words as viciously as her position permitted.

By this time the village policeman had arrived on the scene. Temple immediately took him aside, and after a minute's confidential talk the officer dispersed the crowd, leaving Temple free to look after Iris.

'How did you get off the train?' he asked her.

'The train stopped at High Moorford. Van Draper and Guest were waiting,' she explained with a twisted grin. 'Hell! This shoulder's worse than I thought.'

Temple surveyed her with a puzzled frown for some moments. She was gingerly moving the fingers of her uninjured hand over the hurt shoulder. She was very badly shaken, and very unlike the old assured Iris. Temple decided that this was a very opportune moment. He began to speak rapidly, in soft, urgent tones.

'Iris, they got you off that train for a very definite purpose. They wanted to make quite certain that you wouldn't talk!'

'Yes! Yes! I know!' cried Iris furiously. 'But, by God, I'll talk now all right!'

Her nerves were obviously keyed to breaking point.

Somewhere in the distance the bell of an oncoming ambulance echoed mournfully.

'Listen, Iris,' said Temple suddenly. 'I'm going to take a chance. Get that shoulder attended to, then meet me at the Shepley Hotel, High Moorford.'

'The Shepley?' repeated Iris rather vaguely. 'What time?'

'Let's see,' he murmured thoughtfully. 'I'm seeing Sir Graham at two . . . better make it five o'clock.'

'Five o'clock. All right!'

He looked at her a little doubtfully.

'Don't worry,' she grimly assured him. 'I'll be there.'

With its bell clanging, the ambulance came alongside. Two men in white coats sprang onto the pavement.

'I'll be there,' she repeated as the door closed.

'I hope so, Iris,' murmured Temple, as the ambulance drove off. 'By Timothy, I hope so . . .'

5

'Was she badly hurt?' demanded Steve anxiously, when Temple rejoined her.

He shrugged his shoulders.

'Nothing very serious. She had a very lucky escape.'

He glanced at the clock on the dashboard.

'By jove, we'll have to move, or we'll be late!'

'The cigarettes . . .' Steve reminded him.

'No time now – we'll get them in High Moorford.'

'What was the matter with Iris' car?' Steve was eager to know.

'She seemed to think it had been "fixed",' he replied noncommittally.

'But, Paul, who would do that?'

'Ah,' grinned Temple enigmatically. 'Perhaps she'll enlighten us when we see her later on.'

'Later on?' said Steve in some surprise.

He guided the car dexterously round a sharp bend.

'Yes, we're meeting at the Shepley Hotel.'

'Do you think she'll be well enough?'

'I have every reason to believe so,' he said.

A few seconds later Temple heaved a sigh of relief; they were on the outskirts of High Moorford.

The Purple Heather Café was the only prepossessing restaurant in the town, and they found Forbes sitting at a table at the far end of a long room, rather impatiently awaiting their arrival. As soon as he saw Temple he pulled a wry face.

'No luck,' he said. 'I'm damned if we can find the chalet.'

'Didn't you say that you were going to put Inspector Sandford on the case?' asked Steve, who had come across Sandford in the days when she was a reporter.

Forbes nodded. 'Sandford's been on the lake since ten this morning. He knows this district like the palm of his hand, but I'm damned if he can drop on their hideout.'

'I suppose you've got someone up at Skerry Lodge?' queried Temple.

'Good lord, yes! The house is practically surrounded – though I'm afraid it's a case of shutting the stable door after the horse has bolted. I've got a man watching Mrs Moffat's shop too, though I've given him strict instructions to keep well in the background. I thought it might be quite a good idea to allow the old girl plenty of rope – if she really is mixed up with this gang – then there's just a possibility that she might lead us to the chalet.'

Temple smiled. 'There's an old saying that if you give a Scotsman enough rope he'll start making cigars! And you can rely on Mrs Moffat to be pretty canny. She's mixed up in this all right, and I have a hunch that when Z.4 does contact the gang, it will be through Mrs Moffat.'

'But how the devil will she recognise Z.4 if they have never met?'

'Quite simple, Sir Graham. Z.4 has obviously supplied Mrs Moffat with some sort of password.'

'I know,' interrupted Forbes irritably. 'But somehow I can't bring myself to believe that the gang are still ignorant of Z.4's identity. Surely by now van Draper must know it – or possibly Guest.'

Temple shook his head.

'No, I don't believe any of them know who Z.4 really is,' he answered decisively.

Forbes shrugged his shoulders helplessly.

'Well, if that's the case, how the devil can Z.4 be absolutely certain that he isn't going to be double-crossed?'

'They can't very well double-cross Z.4 if they don't know who Z.4 really is,' Steve pointed out, with a flicker of amusement.

'I don't mean it in that sense, Steve. What I mean is, that they could refuse to take the slightest notice of Z.4's instructions if—'

'And so they would,' interposed Temple, 'if it wasn't for that one little factor you seem to be overlooking – blackmail!'

Steve stirred her coffee reflectively.

'You said yourself, Sir Graham, that Z.4 knew something about each member of the organisation,' she reminded him.

'That was only a theory, Steve,' said Forbes. 'And I'm beginning to doubt if it was a very sound one.'

'On the contrary, Sir Graham,' put in Temple calmly, 'the theory was excellent.'

Forbes sat up abruptly.

'What makes you so certain?' he demanded curiously.

'Merely the fact that I happened to discover the little something that Iris was hoping to conceal and that she felt sure only Z.4 knew about.'

He looked round as if to make sure there was no possibility of their being overheard. Then he leaned across the small table.

'You remember the telegram I received?'

Forbes pursed his lips and nodded.

'"Hotel Martinez . . . Nice . . . April 14th, 1932",' he quoted. The Chief Commissioner still retained the habit of committing data of potential importance to memory.

'Well, that telegram proved to Iris beyond a shadow of doubt that Z.4 was not the only person who knew her secret.'

'All the same, she didn't talk – in spite of the telegram.'

'No,' said Temple, 'she didn't talk – then. But I think she will.'

'Well, we shall hear all about that when we get Iris to Glasgow,' replied Forbes sceptically.

'Paul, you're being very mysterious about your precious telegram,' said Steve. 'What exactly did it mean?'

'Yes, I've been wondering about that, Temple,' said Forbes. Temple beckoned to the waitress and asked her to get him some cigarettes.

'Yes, Sir Graham, when you told me that, in your opinion, Z.4 had some sort of hold over each member of the organisation, I made up my mind to discover just what it was that Iris was anxious to conceal.'

'And did you?' asked Forbes rather eagerly.

Temple smiled.

'In nineteen thirty-two Iris married a young stockbroker by the name of Forrester. They spent their honeymoon – or part of it – at the Martinez Hotel in Nice. On April the fourteenth, two days after they had arrived at the hotel, Forrester was found dead. To all intents and purposes it was suicide. But—'

Forbes leaned forward expectantly.

'Yes, Sir Graham, there was a "but", and a rather unpleasant one, I'm afraid, so far as Iris was concerned.'

'But, damn it all, Temple,' said Forbes, 'surely we'd have heard about this. Iris Archer isn't exactly a nonentity.'

'Not at the present time,' Temple admitted. 'But in nineteen thirty-two Iris was known by the somewhat more fanciful name of "Rosie Shiner".'

'Rosie Shiner?' repeated Forbes, thoughtfully probing his memory.

'But what happened about Forrester?' asked Steve.

Temple took several press cuttings from his wallet and scanned them casually.

'The whole business as far as I can gather from the French authorities – and also from these clippings – is a bit of a mix-up,' said Temple. 'Iris wasn't actually accused of the murder, but the authorities had a nasty sort of suspicion that she was mixed up in it. The most important witness, however – an English chambermaid who happened to be working at the hotel – suddenly disappeared, and after a short while the matter was more or less dropped.'

'M'm . . .' grunted Forbes. 'Well, all this certainly seems to do away with the suspicion that Iris might be Z.4.'

'Iris isn't Z.4, Sir Graham,' Temple quietly assured him. 'I'm certain on that point.'

'Then who the devil is?' queried Forbes irritably. 'D'you reckon it's Steiner?'

'But we know who Steiner is, don't we, Sir Graham?' asked Temple innocently. 'He's a Professor of Philosophy at the University of Philadelphia.'

'M'm ...' murmured Forbes sceptically.

He had to admit that he had made no progress with the mildly pleasant Austrian, though he had engaged him in conversation on several occasions. These talks had consisted mainly in endless inquiries from Steiner on the subject of the criminal mind. Forbes had done his best to answer the pertinent questions, but his many efforts to sidetrack the conversation to such subjects as Steiner's private life had met with almost conspicuous failure. Doctor Steiner had proved himself adept at the delicate art of begging the question.

The Chief Commissioner abruptly stubbed out his cigarette in an ashtray.

145

'Of course, there's Rex Bryant,' he said. 'I'm damned if I can make Bryant out, Temple.'

'Yes, after all, we did find his watch chain on Ernie Weston,' said Steve. Nevertheless, she was reluctant to throw any suspicion on the colleague of her reporting days.

'That isn't necessarily an indication that Bryant was implicated – in Weston's murder, I mean,' put in Temple quickly.

'Good heavens, Temple, he must be mixed up in this business somehow or other!' snapped Forbes. 'Otherwise how the devil did Weston get hold of the watch chain in the first place?'

'I don't think there's any doubt about that,' replied Temple imperturbably. 'He helped himself to it. Just as he helped himself to Steiner's cufflinks and Lady Retford's ring.'

'Lady Retford's ring?' echoed Forbes in bewilderment.

'How do you know the ring belonged to Lady Retford, darling?' asked Steve.

'I made inquiries at the local police station. Quite an obvious procedure, eh, Sir Graham?' Temple grinned mischievously. 'They told me that Lady Retford stayed at the "Royal Gate" about a fortnight ago. She was only there for a week, but Ernie managed to get hold of the ring all right. Poor old Ernie was an opportunist, if nothing else.'

Forbes took out his pipe and began to fill it.

'Yes, but what the devil does all this prove?' he demanded. 'Merely that Ernie Weston was a sort of common pickpocket.'

'It certainly doesn't explain the identity of Z.4,' said Steve.

'And another thing, Temple,' Forbes persisted, 'if Weston was just an ordinary little kleptomaniac and didn't have a row with Rex Bryant, and wasn't mixed up with all this other business – who the devil killed him?'

'Z.4,' answered Temple, carelessly dropping his cigarette end into his coffee cup.

'But why? In heaven's name . . . why?'

'Your guess is as good as mine, Sir Graham,' said Temple calmly. He deftly extracted another cigarette from the packet.

'But what is your guess, Temple?'

Temple picked up a match, surveying it intently for a moment, then lit it by scratching it with his fingernail.

'My guess is this,' he proceeded rather more seriously. 'The moment I arrived at the inn, Weston went through my pockets and found the letter that Lindsay – or Hammond if you like – had given me. Later, realising that the letter might be of some personal value to me, he returned it. You may remember that the letter was pushed under the door.'

Forbes was nervously cramming the charge of tobacco into his pipe.

'Yes, but that doesn't explain why he was murdered,' he pointed out.

'Doesn't it?' smiled Temple. 'Well, this is my theory, Sir Graham. After he had returned the letter, the poor devil must have mentioned the fact to someone, and unfortunately for him that someone happened to be Z.4. Naturally, Z.4 wanted the letter before it got into your hands. It was, in fact, absolutely imperative that Hammond's message shouldn't reach you. And yet Ernie Weston, after having had possession of the letter, had calmly returned it. By Timothy, you can imagine how Z.4 felt about it!'

'My God, yes! It's certainly a motive,' admitted Forbes with some emphasis.

'But Weston couldn't have known anything at all about Z.4, or he'd have understood the message,' Steve interjected.

'Exactly,' nodded Temple.

Forbes was obviously intrigued.

'Look here, Temple! Supposing Bryant started questioning Weston about the watch chain. Weston got a bit nervous,

began to suspect Bryant was some sort of police officer, and
without thinking started telling him about the letter. Bryant
would naturally put two and two together and—'

'The same thing applies to Doctor Steiner, Sir Graham,'
Steve interrupted excitedly. 'He may have questioned Weston
about his cufflinks. Weston may have broken down as you
suggest, and then, without realising its significance, mentioned
the letter. Incidentally, Steiner could have been responsible
for Bryant's watch chain disappearing; planting it on Weston
in order to throw suspicion on to Bryant.'

'By Timothy, we'll make a detective of you yet, Steve!'
smiled Temple.

'Thank you, darling,' she replied demurely.

'Seriously, Temple, don't you think Steiner is Z.4?' asked Forbes.

Temple, who had been listening to the others' theories
with just the merest flicker of a smile round the corners of
his mobile mouth, pushed back his chair.

'I think it's about time we got back to the "Royal Gate",
Sir Graham,' he answered pleasantly. 'Perhaps Sandford has
some news by now.'

Forbes looked at him shrewdly for a moment, then gathered
up the check which lay on the table, produced some loose
change and beckoned to the waitress. They rose and began to
put on their coats. Adjusting his scarf to his satisfaction, Forbes
suddenly remarked: 'I see the *Golden Clipper* had a pretty rough
trip the other day. What was it like when you came across?'

'Perfect,' said Steve. 'We enjoyed every minute of it, didn't
we, Paul?'

'Every minute,' the novelist corroborated.

Forbes sighed.

'I wish to God I could get away for a month or so. Never
been to the States.'

'You'd love it,' enthused Steve, extracting her gloves from her husband's overcoat pocket.

'Oh well, we might think of it in about a couple of years,' said Forbes, as they came out of the café and stood in the pleasant afternoon sunshine. 'I've always wanted to travel. As our friend Mrs Moffat would say, "What was it Shakespeare said about travellers?" Is that your car over there, Temple?'

But Temple did not seem to hear him. He stood staring quite vacantly away beyond the roofs of High Moorford to the purple-blue mountains in the distance.

'What is it, darling?' asked Steve, gripping his arm.

'Did Mrs Moffat use those actual words, Sir Graham – "What was it Shakespeare said about travellers?"'

'Why, yes . . .' answered Forbes a little uncertainly.

'When? When did she say it?' insisted Temple, more urgent now than he had been in the restaurant.

'Why, the first time I went into the shop,' replied Forbes. 'But I can't for the life of me see what you're driving at.'

'By Timothy, what a fool! What an utter fool!'

'Darling, what is it?' asked Steve anxiously.

'Don't you see?' Temple brought his gloved fist into the palm of the other hand. 'Mrs Moffat said exactly the same thing to me. "What was it Shakespeare said about travellers?" If I had given the right answer – or if you'd have given it, Sir Graham – *she'd have thought we were Z.4!*'

'My God!' ejaculated Forbes, patently staggered. 'You mean that's the password?'

But Temple was once more busy with another train of thought.

'Travellers . . .' he was muttering to himself. 'What is the quotation? Do you remember it, Steve?'

She shook her head. He turned to Sir Graham, but found no assistance. Then Steve pointed to a bookshop a little farther down the street, and Paul Temple smiled.

A very polite elderly gentleman came to meet them.

'Have you such a thing as a book of Shakespearian quotations?' asked Temple.

The elderly gentleman shook his head.

'I'm afraid there's not much call for it, sir,' he murmured regretfully. 'Now we've several Burns' quotations . . .'

'I'm afraid it must be Shakespeare,' replied Temple firmly. 'Unless you happen to have a book of classical quotations . . . ?'

'Why, yes, I believe we have,' said the shopkeeper with the vagueness common to most keepers of bookshops. He switched on the light in a dark corner of the shop, and after a short interval emerged with a bulky volume.

'This is the only one we have, sir. I'm afraid it's ten and six—'

'Might I just look through it?' asked Temple.

'With pleasure, sir.'

Temple turned the pages eagerly. Suddenly he stopped, thrust the money into the rather bewildered shopkeeper's hand, and seized Steve's arm. A few seconds later they were on the pavement with Sir Graham.

Temple reopened the book at the place he had marked and read:

'"Travellers ne'er did lie – though fools at home condemn 'em".'

Forbes looked at Steve and shrugged his shoulders helplessly.

But Temple seemed to have forgotten their very existence.

'"Though fools at home condemn",' he murmured to himself. 'If only I'd thought of it! By Timothy, if only I'd thought of it!'

6

The plain-clothes man who had been detailed to keep an eye on Mrs Moffat's shop was feeling more than a trifle bored. So far, he had seen nobody go into the shop but the villagers. At least, he could not imagine them as anything but honest-to-goodness homely Scots. Women in shawls mostly. He was surprised that they never seemed to remain very long in the little shop; just time enough to conduct some humble transaction. Either they were very busy folk in the village, he reflected, or Mrs Moffat did not encourage them to gossip. This was the only unusual feature of the plain-clothes man's vigil up-to-date.

It wasn't too easy watching any particular objective in this tiny village, particularly in broad daylight. Strangers were naturally conspicuous amongst such a small population, and the plain-clothes man felt he was already attracting far too much attention. He was thankful when the small public house almost opposite Mrs Moffat's opened its doors, and he was able to continue watching from the comparative comfort of its bar parlour. Having imbibed three glasses of extra strong Highland Ale, he was feeling rather more pleased with the world and rather less conscientious about his duties, when he heard a car stop outside. This was something of an event in the quiet little hamlet, and he felt bound to investigate.

The plain-clothes man saw two men leave the car and enter the shop. He did not know them, but took a mental note of their appearance. He also went to some trouble to commit the number of the car to memory.

Mrs Moffat seemed to be expecting them, for she at once beckoned them into the room at the back of the shop.

'Ye mustn't stay many minutes,' she informed them. 'There's a man watching the place.'

Guest recoiled in some alarm.

'It's all right,' she smiled. 'The nearest telephone is half a mile away from here, so it'd be quite a while before he could get a message through.' She indicated two vacant chairs.

'What happened about Iris?' she inquired.

'It came off all right,' Guest told her. 'We've just passed her car halfway through a shop window. Must have been a hell of a smash . . . they told us she'd been taken to hospital nearly dead.'

Mrs Moffat shook her head almost sorrowfully. 'She was a bonnie lass – and useful, too. But Z.4 can take no chances.'

'Have you heard from Z.4?' asked Guest, a note of eagerness creeping into his voice.

'Not yet.'

Van Draper pushed his chair back so that it grated disagreeably on the stone flags. 'The screen is completed,' he growled. 'Hardwick's ready for him. Why the devil doesn't he come out into the open?'

'Don't worry – he will,' Mrs Moffat calmly assured him.

'He?' Guest took her up at once. 'Has it occurred to you that Z.4 might be a woman?'

Both men looked at her keenly, but she betrayed no sign.

'Perhaps,' she murmured, without a trace of emotion in her voice.

'Well,' said Guest, rising and nervously pacing up and down the kitchen, 'the sooner this business is all wound up, the better I'll like it. The police have been searching for the damned chalet all day long. It's getting too warm to be pleasant.'

'Don't worry, they won't find the chalet very easily,' said Mrs Moffat.

'I know that. But Hardwick is getting disagreeable again.'

Mrs Moffat shrugged her shoulders. 'Can't two of ye keep a wee man like that quiet?'

Van Draper spread his hands over the small fire that burned in the grate. 'There's one thing we do know,' he murmured reflectively. 'Once Z.4 does come out into the open, the financial side of the business must be pretty well cleared up. He isn't making a move until he's absolutely certain there's a market for the screen – that's obvious.'

'There's no lack of markets,' said Mrs Moffat. 'Practically every country in Europe has been bitten by the rearmament bug.'

No one spoke for a few moments.

'You seem pretty well informed, Mrs Moffat,' commented van Draper, eyeing her curiously.

'Of course I'm well informed,' she retorted. 'I use my own common sense.'

'I see,' said van Draper. He could not quite make up his mind whether to confront Mrs Moffat openly with being Z.4. But eventually he thought better of it.

'Come along, Guest. We'd better get back to the chalet,' he declared abruptly, picking up his gloves.

Guest nodded. At the door he turned towards Mrs Moffat.

'The moment Z.4 arrives—' he began, rather nervously.

'The moment Z.4 arrives, we shall both come down to the chalet,' she calmly informed him.

The door closed on the visitors. From the public house opposite the plain-clothes man watched them go. They had been there eleven minutes by the bar parlour clock. He felt he had earned another glass of extra strong Highland Ale, but instead of ordering the drink he left the inn and made his way towards the two-seater Morris that was waiting for him at the back of Mrs Moffat's shop. As he passed the public house and made for the open road he caught a glimpse of Rex Bryant on the verge of entering the shop.

'Good afternoon,' said Rex pleasantly, as Mrs Moffat came out of the kitchen.

'Good afternoon, what can I get you?' she demanded almost in one breath.

Rex looked round the shop, taking in its varied stock. Little escaped him, for it was almost second nature for him to observe these things. He could have written a bright half-column on this village emporium straight onto his typewriter without even pausing to cogitate. Sometimes he despised this sixth sense of his, calling it a "photographic mind", but he had to admit that it had frequently been useful to him.

'I want some razor blades,' he said, smiling disarmingly. 'Got any "Pride of the Regiment"?'

'No, I'm afraid I haven't,' Mrs Moffat replied almost mechanically, for she was studying Rex closely rather than paying any attention to what he was saying.

'Good lord, you should always keep a stock of "Pride of the Regiment",' Rex told her. 'Wouldn't shave with anything else. Makes your face as smooth as a baby's—' He broke off suddenly from this light bantering to observe. 'I say, old girl, you'll know me the second time and no mistake.'

'You've been here before, haven't ye?' she said slowly.

'Yes, once or twice. I always patronise the small trader,' smiled Rex.

'Where do ye come from now?' asked Mrs Moffat.

'Where do I come from now?' grinned Rex, sketchily mimicking her dialect. 'I come from Chelsea, Mrs Moffat. Gay old Chelsea. Where girls are girls and men are . . . well, that's a moot point.'

'Chelsea?' she repeated. 'That'd be a long way I'm thinkin'.'

'You think quite rightly,' he laughed. 'It's fairly near a place called London.'

'I've a married sister in London. Peckham, I think it is. Is there a place called Peckham?'

'Yes,' said Rex, 'there is a place called Peckham.'

Mrs Moffat sighed.

'It must be a wonderful thing to travel,' she said. 'Often wish I had the time. And the money, of course. What was it Shakespeare said about travellers?'

Rex Bryant picked up a packet of cheap razor blades from off the counter.

'I think the exact words were: "Travellers ne'er did lie, though fools at home condemn 'em".'

He looked at the packet, then placed sixpence on the small rubber mat. 'Travellers . . . ne'er . . . did lie . . .!' he murmured, almost to himself. He looked up to find Mrs Moffat staring full into his eyes.

'Z.4!' she breathed in mingled tones of awe and reverence.

CHAPTER VI

Introducing Z.4

1

With Guest at the wheel, the car shot away from Mrs Moffat's shop, and was soon bumping over the rough Highland road, with moorland sweeping away to the horizon on either side. For quite a while neither man spoke, each being busy with his thoughts. In situations like this van Draper was far more ruthless than Guest, whose nerves had suffered badly in the war.

Laurence van Draper betrayed not the slightest trace of nerves as he lit a cigarette and asked: 'How far would it be now, Guest?'

'We haven't reached Aberford yet,' replied Guest irritably.

'All right,' grinned van Draper, 'I never know my whereabouts in these damned moors and mountains. Give me the cities every time.'

Guest made no reply.

Van Draper lowered the window to throw out the match.

'I shall be interested to know what's happened to Iris,' he said thoughtfully.

'I shouldn't imagine Iris would get very far – after the way her car was fixed,' said Guest, looking straight ahead.

'We must buy a paper in Aberford. That might tell us something.'

'H'm,' muttered Guest sceptically, for he didn't see how the papers could print the story as quickly as all that. Of course, the fact that Iris was a famous actress might speed things up, particularly if she had been killed. Some local correspondent would probably be making a small fortune out of 'linage'.

'I hope to God everything is all right at the chalet,' said Guest in rather a worried tone.

Van Draper looked surprised. 'What do you mean?' he asked.

'Hardwick was pretty furious when we left,' Guest reminded him. 'He was beginning to realise—'

'Don't worry, he'll be there all right,' replied van Draper with a chuckle. 'Houdini himself couldn't have wriggled out of that position.'

He laughed again at the recollection of the scene, but this laugh suddenly stopped short.

'What is it?' asked Guest, sensing that something was wrong.

Glancing into the driving mirror, van Draper had caught a glimpse of a black saloon car which he had noticed on the main road some distance back. They were on a side road now, and one that was very little frequented. Could the black saloon be following them?

'That car behind,' said van Draper rather abruptly.

'What about it?' asked Guest, looking into the mirror.

'I saw it before on the main road. I didn't think they'd follow along here ...'

He turned in his seat and for two or three minutes gazed intently at the road behind. 'Yes, he's on our tail all right,' he decided at last.

'What are we going to do?' asked Guest, nervously licking his lips.

'Keep your head,' snapped van Draper, looking round again. 'There only seems to be one man inside, and we can deal with him all right.' He looked back again as the pursuing car came a little nearer.

'Van, we can't do much more on this road,' said Guest, as they bumped along at nearly fifty miles an hour.

'Very well – slow down,' ordered van Draper. 'When he gets level with you, force him over to the side.'

'But, Van, we can't possibly—'

'Do as I say!' shouted van Draper, suddenly very angry. In situations like this he was used to taking command.

Guest gritted his teeth. 'All right – you've asked for it!' he replied, as he took his foot off the accelerator. During the next hundred yards the approaching car drew level. Guest drew well into the side of the road. When the bonnet of the second car was right at their side van Draper suddenly called out: 'Let him have it ... NOW!'

Guest wrenched at the wheel, and the pursuing car bounced away from them as a rugby footballer hands off an opponent. But they had forgotten that their pursuer's speed was greater than theirs, and they suffered even more from the impact.

'Look out!' cried van Draper. 'He's skidding.'

'My God!'

The cars collided with far greater force than they anticipated, and the shock sent each of them into the ditch on opposite sides of the road. Guest heard the windscreen splinter, felt the driving wheel smite him in the chest, then remembered nothing else.

When he recovered consciousness some time later he could see that the driving wheel had saved him from the fate of van Draper, who had been flung towards the windscreen.

For a moment Guest could hardly believe it. Gingerly he felt himself all over, then dragged himself towards van Draper.

'Van . . . are you all right?' he cried in a hoarse voice that he hardly recognised as his own.

'Van! Van!' he called desperately, and shook the inert form. Suddenly realising that van Draper was dead, Guest came very near to panic. Feverishly he searched in a cubbyhole under the windscreen and found a small flask of brandy. After taking a long pull he felt much better.

Then he thought of the other car. What if the man had escaped and was waiting for him?

But there was no sign of life.

Guest went up to the other car and saw that the driver had been flung against the side window. He had received a severe blow on the head, which was badly cut. The car, however, seemed to be far less damaged than his own. Guest looked desperately in all directions. Someone might come along at any minute.

His brain began to work swiftly. By a tremendous shove he managed to restore the Morris to an even keel. Then he started the engine. After a slight pause he lifted out the inert body and laid it on the roadside.

Just as he was about to climb back into the car Guest paused, then went over to the body of van Draper. Without stopping to discriminate, he thrust all the letters and papers he found into his own pockets.

He carefully backed the police car onto the road again and headed for the chalet.

2

'Yes,' said Rex Bryant evenly, 'Z.4 ...'

He looked Mrs Moffat straight in the eyes and favoured her with a smile that had gained him many an interview from unwilling politicians.

For once Mrs Moffat betrayed her excitement.

'We've been waiting for ye! My God, how we've waited! I was beginning to think ye'd leave it too late,' she said.

'Can't we go into the back parlour?' said Rex. 'It's rather difficult talking here.'

'Why, yes, of course!' She nodded eagerly, and was about to lead the way. Then she paused and went to the shop door, which she bolted carefully top and bottom. 'Mind the first step,' she adjured, 'it's a bit tricky in the dark ...'

Rex followed her into the back room.

She turned and faced him.

'We followed out your instructions about Iris,' she rapidly informed him.

'About Iris?' repeated Rex, slightly bewildered.

'Why, of course – about Iris and the car.'

'Oh yes,' said Rex, recovering his composure, 'about Iris and the car . . . now let's see—'

'But surely you remember,' said Mrs Moffat, somewhat puzzled.

There was hardly a noticeable pause before Rex said: 'Yes, yes, of course, I was thinking of something else.' As an afterthought, he added: 'How is Iris?'

'We haven't heard,' said Mrs Moffat quietly. 'Not yet.'

'Oh,' said Rex blankly. 'I see. And Hardwick?'

Mrs Moffat took a deep breath.

'The screen is finished,' she told him.

'Good,' said Rex.

'And how are things at your end?' Mrs Moffat demanded rather nervously. 'Are the arrangements complete?'

'Yes,' said Rex, taking out a cigarette. 'Quite complete. Did you have much trouble with Hardwick?'

'Not at first. He was too bitter about things. Now he seems rather difficult.'

'Difficult?'

'Yes. At times he gets almost violent. The poor devil can't understand why we moved him to the chalet.'

'No,' said Rex, 'I suppose he can't.' He blew out a cloud of smoke, then asked as casually as possible: 'How far do you reckon the chalet is from here?'

'How far?' echoed Mrs Moffat, surprised. 'But ye know where the chalet is as well as I do!'

'Of course,' replied Rex easily, 'but I've never been there.'

'Never been there! But ye had the place made ready for us!' cried Mrs Moffat. 'It was ye who—'

She broke off in obvious alarm. Her placid features had lost their immobile expression. Her mouth was twitching with obvious excitement.

'My God! You're not Z.4!' she gasped.

Rex threw his half-smoked cigarette into the fireplace.

'I'm sorry to disappoint you, Mrs Moffat, but you are quite right. I am not Z.4,' he said calmly.

She made a sudden movement in the direction of the door. 'Stand away from that door!' he ordered sharply. His right hand was in his coat pocket. 'If I were you, Mrs Moffat, I should sit down,' he advised. 'I'd hate to spoil this perfectly good suit by shooting through the coat pocket.'

Mrs Moffat relapsed onto a nearby chair.

'Who are you?' she mouthed. 'Who the devil—'

'All in good time, Mrs Moffat, all in good time,' he cut in curtly.

Then his eye caught sight of a telephone standing on a side table.

'Is that switched through?' he asked.

She nodded without speaking.

Rex went over and picked up the receiver.

'Hello . . . Inverdale 83, please . . . yes, 83 . . .'

He placed a hand over the mouthpiece and turned to Mrs Moffat again. 'Now, Mrs Moffat, perhaps you'll have the goodness to tell me more about the chalet.'

She shook her head. 'I'll tell ye nothing.'

'My dear Mrs—' Rex was beginning, when he broke off. 'Hello . . . Inverdale 83? Is that the "Royal Gate"? . . . Will you get Mr Temple at once? . . . Yes, Mr Paul Temple . . . All right, I'll hold the line.'

He turned to Mrs Moffat once more.

'There's nothing like patience, is there, Mrs Moffat?' he demanded cheerfully. 'Nothing like patience . . .'

3

The lounge of the 'Royal Gate' Hotel opened directly from the entrance hall, and was really little more than a glorified sitting room. There were the usual reproductions of Highland pictures. In fact, it was very like the lounge of dozens of private hotels in Kensington and Bloomsbury.

However, the armchairs were comfortable, and Paul Temple and Steve often sat there after meals. They were gossiping idly with Sir Graham when the latter suddenly yawned and stretched himself.

'I'm expecting a telephone call from Wright,' he told them. 'Otherwise I'd go to my room and snatch forty winks.' The

Chief Commissioner looked tired, for he had been getting rather less than six hours' sleep in each twenty-four of late.

'Who's Wright, Sir Graham?' Steve wanted to know.

'The fellow I've got watching Mrs Moffat's place,' he told her.

'Oh, yes,' said Temple, suddenly alert, 'I'd almost forgotten about him.'

Steve, who was facing the door, looked up suddenly to see rather a strange figure framed in the doorway. It was Mrs Weston, wearing outdoor clothes, which gave her an unfamiliar appearance. Her coat was sensible, and if her hat was not in the current fashion, it seemed to suit her. Steve noticed that she wore black stockings and neat shoes, which were nevertheless well adapted for walking Highland roads.

'Going out, Mrs Weston?' asked Steve, finding it difficult to conceal the surprise in her voice. Somehow, one never imagined Mrs Weston going far beyond the 'Royal Gate'. That was her domain, and it took her all her time to look after it.

'Ay, just down to the village,' Mrs Weston nodded.

'It'll be a nice walk,' smiled Steve pleasantly.

'It doesn't look too bright to me,' replied Mrs Weston dubiously. 'There's a mist coming down the mountain.'

'Don't worry,' said Steve, 'it'll keep fine all right.'

'Well, I do hope so, I'm sure,' said Mrs Weston diffidently. At that moment the young man who had taken Ernie Weston's place as porter and man-of-all-work came to the door.

'What is it, Alec?' asked Mrs Weston.

'Telephone,' answered Alec laconically.

'Didn't you find out who it was for?'

He seemed bewildered by her query, and with a muttered exclamation she went to the telephone.

'Looks like your call, Sir Graham,' said Steve, and he rose. But Mrs Weston returned to inform them: 'It's for Mr Temple.'

'Thanks,' said Temple in a toneless voice, and went out to the tiny office across the hall.

'Ah well, I'd better be off,' said Mrs Weston. 'I think mebbe I'll take my umbrella after all, just to be on the safe side.'

They could hear her ferreting in the large iron umbrella stand outside.

'Mrs Weston seems to have taken things rather well, doesn't she?' commented Sir Graham casually.

'Yes,' agreed Steve. 'She does rather ...'

It hadn't occurred to her before.

'I wonder what she really thinks about all this,' went on Forbes. 'After all, when two men are murdered under your very nose as it were – and one of them happens to be your husband into the bargain, then surely—'

A warning cough from Steve brought his speculations to a conclusion. He swung round to see the huge form of Doctor Steiner in the doorway.

'Good afternoon, Mrs Temple,' smiled the Austrian. 'Good afternoon, sir.'

'Good afternoon,' answered Forbes without enthusiasm. 'Just out for a stroll?'

'*Ja,*' Steiner nodded with a twinkle in his eye. '*Ja wenn man ein bischen dick ist muss man abend spazieren gehen ...*'

'And what does that mean, Doctor?' asked Steve, who found herself liking Steiner, in spite of the atmosphere of suspicion that surrounded him.

'It means,' replied the professor, 'that when one is fat one should take plenty of exercise.'

Sir Graham grunted. He had hoped it would mean something rather different.

Steiner turned to go. 'We shall meet later, I hope . . . at dinner?'

'Of course,' said Steve.

'Then for the time being – *auf wiedersehen.*'

'Auf wiedersehen,' she smiled.

Forbes watched him go with a thoughtful frown.

'I'm damned if I can make head or tail of that fellow,' he told Steve, with some exasperation in his voice.

Steve smiled to herself.

Somehow, she could not believe that Doctor Steiner was a hardened criminal.

The Chief Commissioner looked up sharply as Temple re-entered.

'Well?'

'That was Bryant,' said Temple quietly. 'He's at Mrs Moffat's.'

'Rex Bryant! What the devil is he doing there?'

'Well, I'm rather afraid I sent him there,' Temple confessed.

'You sent him?' echoed Sir Graham in mingled surprise and indignation.

Temple nodded.

'But, darling, why?' asked Steve.

Temple resumed his seat and leaned forward eagerly.

'Immediately I realised that we knew the true significance of the quotation – in other words, the means by which Z.4 intended to contact the organisation – I telephoned Bryant.'

'What was the point in that?'

'I instructed him to visit Mrs Moffat's, and by means of the quotation pass himself off as Z.4.'

'Then Rex isn't Z.4?' said Steve at once.

'Of course not.'

'Well, what's happened?' asked Forbes.

Temple became more serious.

'I was hoping,' he continued, 'that Mrs Moffat might be completely taken in by Rex, and divulge the exact whereabouts of the chalet. Unfortunately, that scheme hasn't worked out quite as well as I anticipated.'

'Mrs Moffat hasn't escaped?'

'Oh no. Rex is taking care of that all right. I lent him a revolver – he said he would be scared stiff to use it, but I expect he looks the part all right.'

'Then there's nothing to worry about,' said Forbes excitedly. 'Z.4 is still bound to contact Mrs Moffat. We'll get Z.4, Temple, if I have to arrest the whole village!'

'I hardly think that will be necessary, Sir Graham.'

Forbes nodded. 'Look here, we'd better join Bryant as soon as we possibly can. For all we know, Z.4 might turn up at Mrs Moffat's while we are hanging around here.'

'I'll leave that to you, Sir Graham,' said Temple, rising. 'I've got an appointment at High Moorford which is rather important.'

'An appointment at High Moorford?' repeated Forbes, who quite failed to see the point in this.

'Yes,' replied Temple. 'With Iris Archer.'

'You're joking!'

Temple shook his head.

'You don't mean to say Iris escaped from the train?'

'I'm afraid so,' said Temple. 'Van Draper and Guest had a car waiting for her. The car was tampered with so that the steering collapsed about twenty minutes after she'd started.'

'Good God! What happened?'

'Fortunately, Iris escaped with a pretty bad shaking. She's meeting me at the Shepley Hotel, High Moorford. That trick with the car didn't exactly please Iris, Sir Graham.'

'You think she'll talk?'

'I'm sure of it.'

The Chief Commissioner was now much more cheerful, and openly delighted with the turn of events. 'Things are looking up, Temple!' he enthused. 'Even if we can't find out about the chalet from Mrs Moffat, we still have another string to our bow.'

'We'll find the chalet all right,' Temple assured him. 'You see, van Draper and Guest visited Mrs Moffat's shop, and according to Rex, who arrived on the scene just as they were leaving, your man is tailing them. That's why he hasn't telephoned.'

'So if van Draper and Guest are on their way to the chalet, Wright can't miss it. Things certainly are looking up!'

'Paul, it's nearly five,' Steve reminded him.

'Yes, of course,' said Temple, moving to the door. 'We'll meet you at Mrs Moffat's in about an hour, Sir Graham.'

'Why at Mrs Moffat's?' asked Steve.

Paul Temple smiled.

'Because Mrs Moffat is expecting Z.4,' he said. 'And I'd rather like to be there when Z.4 arrives!'

4

John Hardwick sat hunched in the chair to which he had been tied and gloomily reviewed the situation. Van Draper and Guest had trussed him so rigorously that he had great difficulty in making the slightest movement.

Suddenly he gave vent to a deep, sarcastic laugh. This was certainly a rather ironical position for him to be in. Here he was with the screen finally completed, and he was tied up like a mummy in full view of his own efforts. Rather wistfully, he eyed the gleaming apparatus, the notebooks and plans scattered over his workbench, and wondered if he would ever use them again.

Guest and van Draper had seemed pretty desperate, but they had not threatened him with death. Obviously they, or this mysterious Z.4 he had heard them mention, hoped to have some future use for him. Otherwise he believed they would have 'liquidated' him without any further ado.

It was rather ironical to reflect that he had completed his final tests that very morning, and was now in a position to put on paper the exact specification of the Hardwick Beam working in conjunction with the screen.

With a grim smile, he congratulated himself that he had not committed quite all the final layout to paper. In this respect he had maintained his usual procedure. True, there were some calculations on scraps of paper in the waste-paper basket that might afford some clue to an expert who also had the plans on the bench.

Blueprints were strewn everywhere. On the working benches, on a table in the corner, even on the floor round his ankles. In the final frenzy of completing the beam, Hardwick had consulted one print after another, hurriedly casting them aside when they had served their purpose.

With a rueful grimace he strained against his bonds. They had omitted to tie his hands together, but the cords were very tight round his arms and body and securely fastened to the back of the chair. After a while he discovered that his left wrist was not fastened so tightly as the right, and eventually he managed to extricate it. Then, in his impatience to free himself completely, he struggled to extract a cigarette lighter from his waistcoat pocket. It took a little time, as the cords passed right over the pocket.

But he got the lighter at last, pressed the spring, and a tiny flame leapt into being. Just as he was applying it to the cord, a spasm of pain, as a result of his cramped position, shot through his hand and the lighter fell to the floor amongst the blueprints.

It was out of reach of his feet, which were tied firmly to the chair. The blueprints smouldered, and a tiny wisp of flame licked round the edges of a large roll. Hardwick strained frantically at the cord round his left arm, but the pain persisted, and it was agony to move.

Two pieces of tracing paper were well alight by now, and in desperation Hardwick flung himself, together with the chair, on top of them, in the hope of smothering the flames. Desperately Hardwick rolled to and fro, coughing and choking ...

Giving the cord of the outboard motor turntable a final flick to set the engine whirring, Guest suddenly caught sight of a wisp of smoke on the other side of the L-shaped lake. The chalet lay right at the other extremity, effectively concealed by a small outjutting headland.

Guest was too worried about recent events to give much thought to the distant curl of smoke. When he was nearly halfway across the lake he noticed that its volume had considerably increased. Even then he had some vague idea that it might emanate from some gorse, which the shepherds were often burning in the hills.

But as Guest steered round the headland he suddenly gave vent to an exclamation, and opened the throttle to the full. The chalet, built almost entirely of wood, was blazing with a fierce crackle that he could hear a quarter of a mile away. Already the roof had caught fire, and the flames were licking round the eaves.

Guest ran the boat almost up to the tiny beach before shutting off the engine, and the prow hissed through the soft shingle. Without waiting to secure the boat, he hastened the two hundred yards to the chalet as quickly as he could. He was not in particularly good condition, and he could feel the blood pulsing through his ears as he came within a few yards of the fire.

A wave of heat swept over him, and its fierce intensity brought him to a halt. Even if help had been at hand, he doubted if it would have been possible to make any impression on the fire. He tried another tack, moving round to the side, hoping that the flames had perhaps a lesser hold on the rear part of the chalet. But he was disappointed, and even as he stepped onto the terrace at the back the roof fell in with the terrifying rumble of a minor landslide.

'Poor devil!' murmured Guest to himself. In his army days he had seen many men die, but in most cases the *coup* had been swift and, he imagined, almost painless. For some unaccountable reason, he found that certain incidents from those futile years of 1914-18 flashed before him as he watched the final phases of the fire.

'Well, that's the end of the Hardwick Screen,' he murmured to himself, and for the first time he asked himself if the world would be any the worse for the loss. He had seen the Prez gun spell swift annihilation to thousands who, but for that invention, would be living today. There was no doubt, reflected Guest, the successful disposal by Z.4 of the Hardwick Screen would certainly have precipitated another war.

'You're a sentimental weakling,' he reproved himself. 'I expect it's just sour grapes, if the truth's known.'

Having eventually decided that it would be impossible to salvage anything from the fire, he turned and slowly retraced his steps to the lake. Despite the stern discipline of his army years, Guest was a rather more humane type than van Draper. As is invariably the case, his extra intelligence was accompanied by a somewhat morbid outlook on life. That Guest was gifted in certain directions there could be no doubt. His knowledge of the Prez gun was quite equal to that of the inventor. He had himself hit upon one or two extra refinements to this terrible weapon, and it was the illegal manufacture of these guns for export which had landed him in the clutches of Z.4.

The death of van Draper had upset Guest rather more than he would have admitted to most people, and although Hardwick had been an awkward devil just lately, Guest wouldn't have wished his worst enemy a death of this description.

He came to the boat, and turned once more to look at the smouldering ruins. All their weeks and months of planning and subterfuge had literally gone up in smoke. And all they had to show for it was a hornets' nest. The police had probably found van Draper by this time, and no doubt they would soon identify him.

After that they would be on the lookout for Z.4, who was supposed to be *en route* to Inverdale. Perhaps, thought Guest, he had better return to Mrs Moffat's.

On second thoughts, however, he decided that it would be better to lie low for a day or two, somewhere within easy reach, and where he was not likely to be conspicuous. There was an hotel in High Moorford that should serve his purpose.

Abruptly, Guest turned his back on the remains of the chalet, in an effort to blot out the feeling of futile despair that was creeping over him.

He picked up the piece of string and passed it round the turntable. The engine came to life for a second, then coughed and was silent. Guest looked at the petrol tank. It was empty.

With an imprecation, he got into the boat and pushed off
with the single oar. The prospect of half an hour's rowing
was not attractive in his present condition. What he badly
needed was a good, stiff double whisky.

5

Guest liked the look of the Shepley Hotel in High Moorford.
It was one of the more dignified type, a medium between
a high-class commercial and semi-luxurious residential. It
would be difficult to imagine anything untoward happening
behind those discreet portals. He had left the Morris in a lane
two miles back, and walked the rest of the journey, carrying
only a small suitcase, which he had transferred to the police
car after the accident.

An elderly reception clerk welcomed him with just the
right touch of deference.

'Good afternoon, sir.'

Guest put down his case. 'Good afternoon. Could I have
a room, please? A single room if you have one. I may be
staying for a day or two.'

The clerk consulted a book.

'Very good, sir. Room fourteen.'

'Thank you,' said Guest. 'And could you let me have a
large double Scotch up there right away? Oh, and I shall
want dinner in my room – about seven-thirty.'

The clerk took a note of this, then touched a bell.

'If you wouldn't mind signing the register, sir,' he murmured
politely, pushing the book towards Guest.

Guest took the pen, and wrote: *Major Guest, London.*

'Thank you very much, Major,' said the clerk. 'The room
is on the first floor.'

Guest followed the young porter who had picked up his case. When they had reached the room he turned and said: 'I ordered a large double whisky. On second thoughts, make it a bottle – and bring a syphon too, will you?'

'Yes, sir.'

Guest sank into a chair and idly unlocked the suitcase. He was looking forward to the drink he had ordered. It had been warm rowing, and his nerves could certainly do with steadying.

After what seemed an age the porter reappeared with a tray on which were a bottle, a syphon and three glasses. Guest gave him a shilling and proceeded to pour out the whisky. He was just lifting the glass to his lips when there was the sound of a key in the lock. The door opened and, to his astonishment, Iris came into the room. Without a word, she closed the door noiselessly behind her.

The actress showed no outward sign of injury. At the hospital they had found that there were no broken bones, but her shoulder had been badly sprained. A young doctor had persuaded Iris to try a new electrical treatment for which apparatus had just been installed, and the result had been quite remarkable. Apart from a certain stiffness, she felt no pain in her shoulder, though the doctor had warned her that she would probably do so the next day if she did not return for further treatment.

Guest set down his glass on the pewter tray.

'What the devil are you doing here?' he gasped.

'Surprised, Major?' demanded Iris, with her insolent stare. She leaned against the door and eyed him deliberately.

'What—what happened?' stammered Guest.

'Don't worry,' she replied sarcastically, 'your little trick with the steering worked all right. There was a most spectacular accident that would have cheered you immensely—drop that gun!'

Her right arm was whipped from behind her back, and Guest let fall the revolver he was drawing from his coat pocket. Iris came forward and picked it up.

'Following instructions to the last,' she said.

'Iris . . . things are serious, damned serious,' said Guest hoarsely.

'Well?'

'After you left us at the station, Van and I went to Mrs Moffat's place; then about two hours ago we went on to the chalet.'

'I don't see that this interests me particularly?'

'We were followed, Iris. They've had a man watching the shop for the past week.'

'Go on,' she told him, carelessly fingering the revolver.

Guest was obviously apprehensive.

'The man caught up with us about a mile from Aberford, and the two cars – My God, what a crash! I thought at first—'

'A dose of your own medicine, eh?' she murmured grimly. 'Well, go on.'

'Van was killed – almost instantaneously, I should imagine. The other fellow was pretty badly cut about, but his car was all right, so I continued the journey alone.'

'To the chalet?'

He nodded.

'When I got to the boat, I noticed some smoke rising round the headland, and by the time I got the boat across Skellydown loch the whole place was practically in ruins.'

'How on earth could that happen?' she asked.

Guest swallowed hard. 'You see, when Van and I received our instructions about taking you off the train at High

Moorford, we left Hardwick at the chalet alone. He couldn't escape – we made certain of that all right, but we never dreamt that he'd set fire to the place.'

'Then what's happened to the screen and the beam? And Hardwick too, for that matter?'

Guest shook his head gloomily.

'I don't think there's any doubt about what happened to Hardwick . . .' he said. 'Standing at the side of the lake,' he continued in almost a whisper, 'staring at what was left of the chalet, I suddenly felt desperate and hellishly scared. I knew that Z.4 was on the verge of contacting Mrs Moffat. I knew that sooner or later van Draper would be found, and the net would begin to tighten. I came back over the lake, and decided to stay here for awhile and wait for things to develop.'

'They'll develop all right,' said Iris softly.

'In a day or two I expect I'll go back to town,' he concluded.

'Will you, Major? That's very interesting.'

There was something in the tone of her voice that made him suspicious.

'What do you mean?' he asked.

'Simply this,' she smiled. 'If it hadn't been for a miracle, I shouldn't be here. You did your damnedest to get rid of me, and I always make a point of paying my debts.'

Her voice was cold, level and calculating.

He looked round nervously.

'You needn't try any fancy tricks,' she advised him.

They looked at each other in silence.

'What are you going to do?' he demanded at last.

She waited another minute before replying.

'Strange though it may seem, Major, I'm going to keep you here until a friend of mine arrives.'

'Friend? What friend?' cried Guest in obvious alarm.

She pushed one of the revolvers into the pocket of her tailor-made costume.

'I think you'll find him excellent company,' she said, prolonging his agony of apprehension. 'I'm referring to Temple.'

She noticed his expression change.

'Paul Temple!' he breathed almost inaudibly. 'Why, you dirty, double-crossing little—'

He made a movement towards her, but for the second time she threatened him with the revolver.

'But, Iris, you can't. . .' he began to protest, but she interrupted him in a voice that was quite relentless.

'Whether you like it or not, Major, you are going to wait for Paul Temple!'

Still pointing the gun at him, she picked up his glass of whisky, drank most of it, and pocketed the key to his room which was lying on the dresser. Then she looked at her watch.

It was five minutes to five.

Almost carelessly she left the room, closing the self-locking door behind her.

On the way out she paused at the reception desk.

'If Mr Paul Temple calls,' she told the clerk, 'would you please show him up to Room Fourteen?'

'There y'are, sir,' said the porter, five minutes later, indicating the door of the room.

Temple knocked twice, but there was no reply.

'I say,' he called after the retreating porter, 'have you a key to this door?'

'Isn't the gentleman in?' asked the porter, returning and fumbling with a bunch of keys.

'I'm not sure,' replied Temple.

'Ah well, we'll soon see,' said the other, inserting a key in the lock.

Temple entered.

At a glance he took in the inert form on the bed, the whisky and glasses . . .

'I expect the gentleman's fallen asleep, sir,' suggested the porter, with a knowing wink at the bottle. 'Should I wake him for ye?'

Temple picked up the tiny blue phial that lay on the tray.

'I think you'd find it rather difficult,' he said.

6

The atmosphere of Mrs Moffat's kitchen parlour could quite justifiably have been described as tense. It was also more than a trifle stuffy, for Paul Temple, Steve, and Sir Graham had been cooped in the parlour with Mrs Moffat for over two hours.

The two men and Steve had been smoking from time to time, and since the room was lighted by an oil lamp this hardly improved matters so far as the ventilation was concerned.

Up till now there had been few customers, and in spite of Mrs Moffat's assurance that they were all villagers, Sir Graham had insisted upon her repeating the quotation. Mrs Moffat's growing irritability was therefore understandable.

Nor was she the only person who was showing signs of impatience. Sir Graham's nerves were plainly on edge, and he jumped visibly every time the shop bell tinkled. Steve, too, was beginning to show the same symptoms. Only Temple appeared outwardly unruffled, in spite of his distressing experience at the Shepley Hotel.

After ordering the porter to summon the police, Temple had rushed downstairs in an attempt to discover some trace of Iris. The reception clerk tried to be helpful, informing him that he had seen Iris depart in the direction of the station. But Temple felt sure that she would be more likely to leave by road, so he waited until the local policeman arrived on the scene, showed his credentials, and requested him to telephone Aberdeen to have all trains and road vehicles searched.

Sir Graham grunted when Temple told him the story.

'I thought you were on a bit of a wild goose chase,' he said.

'Nothing of the kind,' Temple disagreed. 'Guest turning up satisfied Iris' lust for revenge. She got even with him. That's all Iris wanted, Sir Graham.'

The Chief Commissioner nodded and paced across the room. Suddenly he turned.

'What time is it, Temple?'

Temple looked at his watch.

'I make it about seven-twenty.'

'That's right, darling,' Steve corroborated. 'I put my watch right by the radio in the car.'

'Heavens, I've been here over two hours!' grumbled Forbes.

'And how much longer do ye intend to stay?' asked Mrs Moffat, who had been maintaining a sullen silence for some minutes. 'Hanging aboot like a lot o' sheep. I'll hae ye know that the shop closes at eight and—'

'I think you know why we are staying, Mrs Moffat,' said Forbes. 'And you might as well make the best of it. We're here until Z.4 arrives.'

'Then for God's sake let's go into the shop,' she snapped. 'We can't all stay in here. If you don't get some air into this room I shall pass out on ye.'

'It is pretty stuffy, Sir Graham,' said Steve.

Forbes nodded. 'I know. But we can see the door from here without being noticed. Besides, the shop must appear to be empty; otherwise Z.4 will never come out into the open.'

'We've no guarantee that he will,' said Temple. 'Recent events might have changed his plans.'

'Yes,' conceded Sir Graham, 'there is that possibility. But somehow I've a feeling that he's going to put in an appearance, and pretty soon.'

Temple lighted another cigarette.

'What happened to Rex, Sir Graham?' asked Steve.

'I sent him back to the inn,' Forbes replied. 'There was no point in Rex staying here. Besides, he was rather anxious to make a start on his story. Maybe he's gone down to the chalet to see if—'

He broke off as the telephone shrilled.

'Hello? . . . Oh, it's you, Murphy. Yes? That's fine . . . good. Well, mind you keep your eyes skinned, and don't hesitate to challenge anybody. It doesn't matter a damn who they are!'

He slammed down the receiver.

'That was one of my men 'phoning from the box down the road,' he explained. 'This shop's guarded like the Tower of London,' he went on excitedly. 'Once we get Z.4 in here he'll never—'

'Sh!' hissed Temple.

The shop door had opened.

'It's Doctor Steiner!' gasped Steve, peering through a little window-like aperture which looked out into the shop.

'You know what to do, Mrs Moffat,' said Forbes in rather a strained voice. 'And don't forget that quotation. There must be no mistake.'

'He's waiting, Mrs Moffat,' said Temple softly.

She favoured them with a hostile look and went into the shop.

'Good evening,' began Steiner pleasantly. 'I should like some postcards, please.'

'Certainly. Would ye like plain postcards or—'

'Picture postcards,' said Steiner, surveying the contents of the little shop with a smile of amusement.

'You're ... you're a stranger round these parts?'

The doctor nodded. 'Very much so, I'm afraid. From Philadelphia, U.S.A.'

'Philadelphia!' exclaimed Mrs Moffat. 'That must be an awful long way?'

'Well, it rather depends where you start from,' said the doctor laughingly. 'Ah, yes. I was forgetting – the postcards. How much?'

'Sixpence.'

'Thank you,' he murmured, as Mrs Moffat handed him the cards.

'Philadelphia,' she repeated, apparently rather entranced by the name. 'It must be a wonderful thing to travel. I often wish I had the time – and the money, of course. What was it that Shakespeare said about travellers?'

Steiner looked at her for a moment, then gave vent to his deep laugh.

'I can't recall offhand, madam,' he replied. 'But I think we can take it for granted that it was not very much to the point.'

He took a handful of small change from his pocket.

'Sixpence, I think you said?'

She nodded.

'Ah, your English coins are so—elusive ...'

He sorted out a sixpence and passed it to her. Rather list-lessly she placed it in the drawer.

Steiner pushed the postcards in his pocket and turned to go.

'Good night, madam,' he said politely.

'Good night.'

The doorbell tinkled once more, and his massive form vanished into the darkness.

'Well, I'm damned!' said Forbes, in such complete dismay that Temple had difficulty in repressing a smile.

Mrs Moffat returned and stood in the doorway, arms akimbo. 'I hope ye're satisfied,' she declared in sarcastic tones. She went to her chair, and relapsed into a brooding silence once again.

A clock outside struck eight.

Mrs Moffat rose.

'I'll be closin' the shop now – or maybe the police will fine me for breaking the regulations.'

'Just a minute, Mrs Moffat,' said Temple, 'I think that clock is five minutes fast.'

With an impatient exclamation, she sat down again. Even as she did so the doorbell rang.

'There's someone else,' hissed Forbes.

Steve peered eagerly through the tiny window.

'Oh, it's only Mrs Weston,' she announced in disappointed tones.

'Now what the devil does she want?' snarled Forbes, who was rather anxious that none of the usual customers should complicate matters by being present in the shop when Z.4 appeared.

Mrs Moffat went into the shop and turned up the oil lamp, which was not quite equal to lighting the gloomy interior.

'Good evening, Mrs Moffat.' Mrs Weston was dressed as she had been when Steve had spoken to her at the "Royal Gate".

'Good evening, Mrs Weston. Shocking weather we're havin'.'

'Ay, I can't remember a worse winter than this, and that's the truth,' replied Mrs Weston, unfastening the top button of her coat. 'We seem to have had nothing but rain since August.' She appeared to be slightly out of breath, and leaned on the counter for a minute to recover herself.

'I was sorry to hear about your husband – it must have been an awful shock to ye,' sympathised Mrs Moffat.

Mrs Weston sighed.

'I don't suppose anyone will ever know just how much I miss him, Mrs Moffat,' she replied with emotion in her voice.

Mrs Moffat nodded sympathetically.

'Oh well,' said Mrs Weston, seeming to pull herself together. 'Now what was it I came in for? Really, my memory's gone from bad to worse. Oh, I remember. I was wondering if you had some sort of a suitcase I could borrow. I've only got one of those old-fashioned trunks, and I'm going down to my married sister's for a few days. I thought the change might take my mind off things.'

'Yes, I think I can help ye,' said Mrs Moffat. 'You wouldn't be wanting to take the case straight away, I suppose?'

'Oh no, there's no great hurry.'

'Then I'll have the boy call round in the morning with it.'

'That would do nicely,' Mrs Weston agreed.

'Is it a long journey ye'll be making?'

'Yes, it's a tidy way. Rotherham. It's near Sheffield, ye know. Have ye ever been to Rotherham?'

'No,' said Mrs Moffat, 'I'm afraid I haven't. There aren't many places I have been to, Mrs Weston, and that's the truth. Often thought I'd like to travel, though – providing, of course, I had the time and money. Now what was it Shakespeare said about travellers?'

Mrs Moffat almost smiled as she spoke the familiar words. Well, they had insisted on it! But to think that a harmless North Country body like Mrs Weston could possibly . . .

183

Suddenly she realised that Mrs Weston was speaking.

A very different Mrs Weston.

Her features had tautened, her voice was cold and relentless.

'Shakespeare said: "Travellers ne'er did lie, though fools at home condemn 'em"!'

Deliberately she repeated the words, until Mrs Moffat's eyes were almost starting out of her head. She stood transfixed, unable to move or speak.

Suddenly the door at the back was flung open and Paul Temple stood framed in the doorway. He was staring at Mrs Weston.

She recoiled a step, and hastily fumbled in her bag.

'Drop that bag, Mrs Weston!' said Temple sharply.

Mrs Weston did not speak. Her usually ruddy features were blanched, her lips drawn to a thin line. The handbag dropped onto the stone floor.

'Come on, Forbes, what are you waiting for?' called Temple over his shoulder.

'But, Temple, you can't mean that Mrs Weston . . .' The Chief Commissioner was obviously perplexed. Temple nodded.

'Permit me to introduce you to the leader of the greatest espionage organisation in Europe,' he said. 'Z.4!'

7

Cosgrove
'Evening Post'
London.
Your blue-eyed boy has turned up trumps again stop arrive Euston midnight stop don't worry about banners bands or red carpet stop clear whole of front page for greatest espionage story of all time stop am bringing

you bottle of your favourite whisky stop.
Rex Bryant.

Bryant
Royal Gate Hotel Inverdale
You're still sacked and I don't drink
Cosgrove.

Cosgrove
'Evening Post' London.
Wish you wouldn't argue stop lay in stock of seventy-two point caps and leave rest to me stop ignore War Office Ministry of Information and any interfering politicians stop first two thousand words from Glasgow in three hours time stop cut a word and I'll murder you stop don't tell chief or he'll panic and consult Churchill stop don't worry it's my favourite whisky too stop.
Rex Bryant.

8

Detective Inspector Wallace Sandford was feeling even more bitter towards the human race than was his usual custom. For well over a week he had been detailed to conduct a search for Iris Archer, and his reports to Scotland Yard could certainly not have been described as enlightening. Of course, he had never seen Iris, which was something of a handicap, but if you had informed Inspector Sandford that a striking blonde, who probably had one arm in a sling, could evade the police resources of the British Isles, he would have indulged in a smile, and perhaps even favoured you with a pitying glance. But there it was. You couldn't get beyond facts.

And the facts were that Iris Archer had promised to meet Paul Temple at the Shepley Hotel, High Moorford. She had certainly visited the hotel, and had even left Major Guest as evidence of the fact.

Actually, Iris had walked out of the hotel, calmly annexed a new American car from just along the street, and driven to Glasgow, where she had left the car in Sauchiehall Street. It had been recovered some six hours later.

But of Iris herself there was no trace. Sir Graham Forbes had issued prompt orders for all the Scottish express trains to be searched, without any tangible result, except that a chorus girl who bore some resemblance to Iris had been temporarily detained at Carlisle, and released again after surprising her captors by the range of her vocabulary.

'I can't understand it at all, Annie,' Inspector Sandford confessed to his wife in the privacy of their trim little villa in an Edinburgh suburb.

At home, he invariably relapsed partly into his native dialect, although when in contact with his superior officers Sandford's English was irreproachably correct. He had been educated at a good secondary school.

His wife, who was placing a huge meal before him, fulfilled her customary role of comforter. 'The lass'll turn up somewhere before long,' she reassured him. 'No woman with a face like those pictures you showed me could hide herself away for long. Some other woman'll be bound to give her away.'

Sandford shook his head somewhat sceptically. 'Don't forget there's been four unsolved murders in the country so far this year,' he reminded her. This was a fact deeply rooted in his subconscious mind.

It was Saturday lunchtime, and he was taking a few hours off for the first time since the search started. Sandford usually enjoyed his lunch on Saturdays because it was invariably a leisurely meal, with a pleasant afternoon and evening to follow.

But his wife took the edge off his appetite in the middle of the first course by announcing that they were paying a visit to her sister in the small town of Craiglea, some twenty miles away.

'But ye know I've got to be on duty tomorrow morning, Annie,' her husband protested. 'Here I've been chasing all over Scotland. I want a bit of peace and quiet.' But Annie waved him aside.

'There's a train soon after nine in the morning, and I promised Susan faithfully that we'd both go. Herbert is particularly looking forward to seeing you.'

Sandford snorted. It wasn't that he hated Susan so much. He could put up with her. It was her husband for whom Sandford had conceived such a hearty dislike. Herbert never seemed to tire of firing off a stream of facetious jokes about the police force. He had a playful habit of greeting his brother-in-law by flinging open the front door and calling over his shoulder: 'They've come for us, Susie. They've found out we aren't married!' Then he would turn to the visitors and declare dramatically: 'It's a fair cop!'

Yes, Herbert had never tired of the novelty of possessing a brother-in-law in the police force, Sandford gloomily reflected, as he helped himself to the last few mouthfuls of his large meal.

Already Annie was bustling about, starting to clear away the things, preparatory to starting for the station. Her husband slowly filled his glass with ale, but the sight of it didn't seem to cheer him as it usually did.

'I canna stick that Herbert,' he muttered. 'He's a sight too smart. Mebbe a week or two in the force would knock some of the clever ideas out of him.'

'You always let him rub you up the wrong way,' Annie protested. 'Anyhow, I promised we'd go,' she declared flatly, and he knew it was useless to argue any further.

To say that Inspector Sandford was disappointed would be putting it mildly. On Saturday afternoons he looked forward to seeing the local amateur rugby club. They were up against a tough proposition this week, and he had been anticipating a lively afternoon. His pals, Geordie Macfarlane and Sandy Lawson, had promised to be there. After the match there would be a game of darts and a drink or two at the 'Golden Thistle'. Sandford had lately become adept at darts, and the game fascinated him. He sighed; today there wasn't even time for him to enjoy his usual after-dinner pipe.

He went up to his room grumbling to himself, and eventually emerged in a blue serge suit, which was far too tight under the arms. Before long his wife joined him, and they managed to catch the three-ten train, which obligingly stopped at every station, landing them at Craiglea at four-fifteen, by which time Sandford had smoked a packet of cigarettes, and was feeling more than a trifle nervy and irritable.

A penny bus ride brought them to their destination, and the front door was opened by Herbert with the usual flourish.

'Susie!' he called. 'There's a plain-clothes cop outside. Quick, old girl, hide the swag!'

Under his breath, Inspector Sandford muttered something which was inaudible. Annie greeted her brother-in-law enthusiastically, and Susie came along the hall to add to the welcome.

'Well, Wally, how's the Big Four these days?' spluttered Herbert, with a knowing wink at Annie. 'When are they promoting you from Scotland to Scotland Yard?'

His brother-in-law did not deign to reply, but Herbert appeared not to notice. 'Hello, you're getting a bit thin on top, Wally. Must have been doing a bit of thinking lately. I suppose you wouldn't have had anything to do with this Z.4 affair that was in all the papers this week?'

'As a matter of fact,' retorted Sandford with ominous deliberation, 'I have!'

For once in a way Herbert was momentarily taken aback. This was the first time he had ever extracted from Sandford any definite acknowledgment that he was connected with certain police activities.

'Well—er—' temporised Herbert, 'not a bad little job, that. Of course, they had to call in that fellow Paul Temple. Do you know Paul Temple by any chance?'

Sandford shook his head and relapsed into the silence he observed for long stretches when visiting his relatives. He noted with satisfaction that there was a huge dish of prawns on the tea table, and found some consolation in this fact; for Inspector Sandford was very partial to prawns.

When they were sitting round the table a few minutes later, Herbert said: 'We've got a surprise for you. Yes, a nice little treat for you this evening.'

'Oh yes,' put in Susan enthusiastically. 'There's a company at the Town Hall this week. I went on Tuesday to see *The Farmer's Wife*, and they were so good that I booked seats for us all tonight.'

'There now,' said Annie, 'I haven't been to a good play for months. But you don't want to see it all over again, do you Susie?'

'Oh, it isn't the same play. They changed it on Thursday. Tonight they're acting a play by Edgar Wallace. I think it's called *The Man Who Changed His Name*.'

'Sounds barmy to me,' commented Sandford sceptically.

'Ah, you don't know it all,' said Herbert. 'Now's your chance to pick up a tip or two, my lad.'

Sandford helped himself to another large portion of prawns without making any further comment. He did not want to start any more silly arguments with Herbert. After all, you can't argue with a fool, he told himself. But Herbert did not intend to let an opportunity like this slip by so easily, and he continued to rally his brother-in-law, to the delight of both women, right up to the end of the meal. When they were all finished, Sandford carefully folded his napkin. Then he took a deep breath.

'One day somebody'll break in and pinch that imitation silver cup you won in the egg-and-spoon race,' he grunted. 'Then you'll run for the police fast enough.'

He knew he touched a tender spot there, for Herbert was very proud of this cup, which, with the help of an extravagant start, he had won in a local hundred yards' handicap, a feat which he had never even remotely approached again.

'I can deal with anybody who breaks into this house,' Herbert snorted, 'and let me tell you that cup's solid silver.'

Sandford grinned for the first time. His shot had struck home. He felt that the afternoon had not been entirely wasted after all.

As there were to be two performances at the Town Hall that evening, and Susan had booked for the first, they had very little time to spare. Also, it was an excuse to hurry the men away from the table before their remarks became even more acidulous. There was, nevertheless, a distinct coolness obvious in the party when they started out, though this wore off a little by the time they had reached the centre of the town.

Craiglea Town Hall had seen better days, but could never have been classed as picturesque architecture. For some peculiar reason, it boasted a tremendous tower, which seemed to serve no purpose whatsoever. And, of course, there was the inevitable balcony, from which election results had been announced since the year the building was first erected.

On two large boards outside, eight-sheet lithographic posters luridly informed the public that the Maxwell Sherwood Dramatic Company presented the sensational crime play: *The Man Who Changed His Name*, 'direct from its phenomenal success at the Regency Theatre, London'.

The entrance was dimly lighted with a row of bare electric bulbs, two of which were not functioning, and the effect was not to be compared with the glaring neon of the majestic cinema opposite. Standing in the vestibule, waiting for Susan and Annie to emerge from the cloakroom, Sandford sighed for the cheery amenities of the 'Golden Thistle'. The Genuine Old Scotch Ale, the darts, the blazing fire throwing a ruddy glow on the faces of the congenial company. And here he was, due to waste the best part of an evening in a musty Town Hall, watching a fourth-rate theatrical company perform an out-of-date detective thriller.

He turned to ask Herbert if the hall had a licence, then paused and finally changed his mind, recalling that Herbert was never very enthusiastic when the question of a 'quick one' arose. 'Maybe I'll be able to slip out during the interval,' Sandford comforted himself. He would certainly need some sort of stimulation to see him through the evening. If it had been the pictures, he could have gone to sleep, but he knew from experience that it would be far too cold in the Town Hall to encourage slumber.

Annie and Susan returned and they entered the main hall. Though they occupied the best seats, these could hardly be described as comfortable, for they were nothing but wooden chairs. Sandford cautiously manoeuvred the party so that he sat on the gangway, with Susan next to him, then Herbert and finally Annie, farthest away so that she would not be able to remonstrate if he went out for a drink, as he fully intended to do.

The solitary piano tinkled out a rough-and-ready overture, which was swallowed in echoes away up in the lofty ceiling. The lights snapped out one by one, and finally the curtain rose rather unsteadily, revealing a dingy box chamber set. On a settee, smoking a cigar, and endeavouring to portray a picture of sinister ease, reclined Maxwell Sherwood himself.

'He's *ever* so good,' Susan whispered to her brother-in-law, who grunted, knowing her childlike worship of make-believe.

'*She's* good, too,' enthused Susan again. 'She was only a maid in the other play, but—'

There were one or two 'Sh's!' from people nearby, so Susan relapsed into silence. Sandford studied the girl on the stage with a thoughtful frown. He had a feeling that he knew the face, that he had seen the girl somewhere before. Herbert leaned across to him.

'What price the red-haired bit, Wally?' he sniggered. His wife silenced him. The play went on, and it became increasingly obvious that the girl with the striking red hair was a more polished performer than her colleagues. Even Sandford realised that she was exploiting an entirely different technique.

Sandford did not leave his seat in the first interval. He stopped and studied the programme, noting that the red-haired girl called herself Lydia Merridew.

Before the lights went down again Sandford took a newspaper cutting out of his pocket and examined it closely. But the photograph, about the size of a postage stamp, was too blurred to convey any adequate impression. The girl in the picture was the most platinum of blondes. He frowned and replaced the cutting in his wallet.

During the second interval Sandford felt he had a legitimate excuse for visiting the 'Town Arms' next door. He leaned across to Herbert and asked: 'Coming?' Rather reluctantly, Herbert followed him.

In the saloon bar of the 'Town Arms' Sandford discovered what he had anticipated. A rather elderly actor, grotesque in his greasepaint, leaning in lordly fashion against the mantel-piece. He recognised him as the butler in the play. Sandford entered into conversation with him almost at once by the simple expedient of standing him a drink.

'How's business?' he asked.

The butler tossed down the drink he had been holding.

'Not bad, old man, not at all bad. Of course,' he added hastily, 'this is only a fill-in, as far as I'm concerned.'

He drew closer to Herbert and Sandford, and continued in a conspiratorial whisper. 'Just between ourselves, this is the first time I've ever been out with a stock crowd. No money in it. But it fills in, old man. It fills in.' He took another pull at his whisky and winked.

'Smart girl you've got in your crowd,' said Sandford casually, 'the red-haired one—'

'Oh, her!' rejoined the butler in the disparaging tone of the small-time professional. 'She only joined last week.'

'Indeed?' said Sandford interestedly. 'Where did she come from?'

'No idea. The old man picked her up somewhere in Glasgow, I believe. They say she took the job for stocking money.' Suddenly the butler caught sight of the clock in the passage outside.

'Hell!' he ejaculated. 'I'm on in two minutes.' He drained his glass at a single gulp and wished them a hasty good night. Sandford suspected that this was merely an excuse to avoid returning his hospitality, but he was not altogether sorry that the man had departed.

'What's all this about that redhead?' asked Herbert curiously as they made their way back to the theatre. 'I thought you had your eye on her. Don't tell me you're starting a new hobby at your time of life!'

'Nothing like that!' snapped Sandford, very much on the alert now. 'You go back in there – I've got a call to make at the police station.'

Herbert looked taken aback for a moment, but did as he was instructed.

Sandford found the station without much difficulty; it was actually very near to the Town Hall. Inside, a burly sergeant was dozing over a huge fire. Sandford knew him by sight, but produced his credentials to save time in any possible argument.

'I want to see all the circulars, photos and any other dope you've got about Iris Archer,' he began briskly.

The sergeant rubbed his eyes, yawned, and went over to some dusty files. Eventually he discovered a photo reproduction and a description. They were not over-methodical at Craiglea.

'Give me a minute or two, and I'll find some more,' the sergeant wheezed. 'There was some stuff came in on Thursday if I remember rightly ...'

'All right,' snapped Sandford, studying the picture, which had been taken two years previously. It was a studio portrait, and the photographer had played tricks with the lighting, with the result that the platinum blonde he had produced might have been any one of the dozen models whom he employed regularly. Sandford was really very little the wiser. The description was the same as that on his newspaper cutting.

'Just give me another minute, Inspector—' the sergeant was mumbling, but Sandford cut him short.

'I want you to help me at the Town Hall. Stand by in case you're needed. And if you bungle things, you'll be losing those stripes of yours!'

By the time they reached the Town Hall the performance was nearly over, and Sandford at once made his way behind the scenes. Mounting some stone steps, he reached the stage level and stood in a corner watching the play. Lydia Merridew was not on the stage. After awhile Sandford approached a scene-shifter and asked: 'Which is Miss Merridew's dressing room?'

'Number Five down the passage,' said the man, with a jerk of the thumb to indicate the direction.

Sandford walked along the corridor and tapped at Number Five.

'Who is it?' said a voice.

'I want to speak to Miss Merridew,' replied the inspector.

The door was opened by the red-haired girl, who had a rather exaggerated make-up. She gave him a searching glance.

'What do you want?'

'I want to talk to you.'

After a pause, during which she scrutinised him shrewdly, she backed a step. 'Better come in.'

He closed the door carefully behind him and looked round the barely-furnished room. Two theatrical baskets stood in one corner, a couple of dresses were suspended on hangers, and the dressing shelf was littered with the usual greasepaints and towels.

'If it's anything private,' said Lydia Merridew, 'you'd better get on with it quickly. I share this room with another girl, and I expect she'll be back in a few minutes.'

She seated herself in front of the mirror and began touching up her make-up. The strong, garish light from four electric bulbs was concentrated on her face. Sandford looked hard into the mirror, and came to a sudden decision.

'I arrest you, Iris Archer, on a charge of attempted murder,' he declared, placing a hand on her shoulder. Under the thin dressing gown she was wearing he felt her wince with a slight exclamation of pain; felt that the shoulder was padded with some sort of bandaging. Then he knew that he had made no mistake.

The eyes in the mirror seemed to be burning into his. After some seconds she turned.

'How in God's name did you find out?' she gasped.

'I haven't the time to go into that now,' he replied sternly.

Sandford had a shrewd idea that she was playing for time, and he had no intention of giving her any loophole.

'You'd better put your coat on and come along,' he ordered brusquely.

'But I can't come like this. I must take my make-up off and change my frock.'

'All right,' agreed Sandford reasonably. 'I'll give you five minutes – and I'll be waiting outside.'

He went back into the corridor and paced steadily up and down. Once or twice a member of the company, leaving or entering a dressing room, eyed him curiously, but he remained quite indifferent.

He gave her seven minutes before tapping on the door.

There was no reply.

'Miss Merridew!' he called sharply.

Still no answer. He turned the knob and found that the door was locked. Without further ado, he flung his full weight against the door. The noise brought several of the actors running out of their dressing rooms.

'What's all this?'

The imperious tones of Maxwell Sherwood resounded along the corridor. 'Look here, my man, you can't—'

'I'm a police officer,' cut in Sandford, gasping from his exertions. 'I've got to get in here.' He continued his assaults on the door, and there was a sudden crash as it gave way. Sandford rushed into the room and over to the far wall. He dragged aside a curtain he had previously noted, imagining that it had concealed some sort of recess. He had been wrong. Behind the curtain was an emergency exit door, leading out to a flight of wooden steps. He was about to descend, when a hand pulled him back.

'Wait a minute!'

It was the elderly butler.

'I noticed this morning the wood in those steps is rotten. Wouldn't stand your weight. Besides, two of 'em are missing.'

Sandford peered out.

In the darkness below, he thought he could discern something white.

'Take me round there – quick as you can!' he ordered.

'Come on,' said the butler, thoroughly enjoying himself. He led the way back through the dressing room, along corridors, down two flights of stairs and into the open.

Iris was lying at the foot of the steps, writhing in pain. One leg was crumpled beneath her.

'Oh, there you are, Inspector,' she said. 'It's my ankle. . . I'd have cheated you if it hadn't been for that damned rotten escape. Might have expected it in a dump like this.'

Sandford turned to the butler. 'Go round to the front and bring the sergeant,' he instructed.

Coming out of the theatre five minutes later, Herbert blinked at the spectacle of his brother-in-law and a burly sergeant assisting a very attractive red-haired actress into a taxi.

Herbert sighed.

'These policemen have all the luck,' he muttered enviously.

9

In one of the first-class compartments of the Coronation Scot three travellers were settling down for the journey.

'We were lucky to get this compartment all to ourselves,' smiled Steve.

Paul Temple laughed.

'Yes, it's wonderful what the police can do, eh, Sir Graham?'

'Well . . .' replied Sir Graham with a twinkle in his eyes, 'this seems to be the first opportunity we've had for talking over the case, so I thought I'd make sure we weren't inter-rupted.' He took out a case of cigars and offered it to Temple.

'Would you care for a cigarette, Steve?' he asked.

'Not at the moment.'

Two minutes later the train slid smoothly away from the platform and clattered through the dingy suburbs. Sir Graham sighed and stretched his legs.

'What happened about your car, Temple?'

'They told me at Aberdeen it'd be through by tomorrow.'

'Not much fun motoring in this weather,' commented Sir Graham.

'No,' said Steve, 'this is much cosier.'

'H'm ...' Sir Graham puffed at his cigar. 'Well, Temple?'

Temple smiled. 'Well, Sir Graham?'

'What puzzles me is that business with Ben. I don't see how the devil you account for—'

'How the devil I account for the flask, Sir Graham?'

'Well, after all, the flask was yours, and there certainly—'

'There was certainly cyanide in the flask,' nodded Temple. 'Yes, I agree. Still, when Mrs Weston sold me that flask I don't suppose she intended that Ben should—'

'Oh, darling!' broke in Steve, horrified.

'Yes,' said Temple seriously, 'that was certainly a lucky escape, Steve, as far as I was concerned.'

Steve pressed his hand, but made no further comment.

'At the time it made me more certain than ever that Steiner was Z.4,' continued Forbes. 'You see, it was Steiner who suggested the drink in the first place.'

'Yes, but Steiner couldn't possibly have known what was in the flask,' Temple pointed out.

'He might have known, Temple,' said Forbes thoughtfully. 'It's very difficult to say. Incidentally, was the flask your first indication that Mrs Weston was implicated?'

Temple shook his head. 'No, the flask merely confirmed what was already in my mind. I had a pretty shrewd suspicion that Mrs Weston had some connection with the affair, even at the very beginning.'

'But, darling, why?' asked Steve.

'Well,' said Temple, 'in the first place, Ernie Weston returned the letter which he had stolen, and which was obviously of supreme importance to Z.4. Shortly after he returned the letter, Weston was murdered. Why? Obviously because he had unwittingly let the cat out of the bag about the letter.'

Light began to dawn upon Sir Graham. 'You mean that he had told his wife about it, without realising that she was Z.4?'

199

'Exactly,' agreed Temple. 'Although, of course, it wasn't quite so simple as that at the time. I knew that he'd told *someone* about the letter, and I was pretty sure that that someone was Z.4. But it might have been Steiner, or possibly Bryant, or possibly some other person we had never even heard of.'

'But, if it was Bryant or Steiner, then Weston must have been on friendly terms with them,' said Forbes.

'That point struck me at once. They must, in fact, have been well aware that Ernie Weston was what is euphemistically termed a kleptomaniac. They must have known, in fact, that he was in the habit of helping himself to other people's possessions. Yet both Bryant and Steiner had been obviously puzzled by the loss of a watch chain and a pair of cufflinks.

'Now, assuming that Steiner and Bryant were all that they seemed to be, or at any rate were not definitely connected with Z.4, then obviously Weston must have spoken to someone else – someone, in fact, who knew exactly the sort of game he was playing. It seemed to me that that someone might very easily be an obvious sort of person after all. A person who Weston really would talk to, without attaching any particular importance to it. Someone, in fact, like his wife . . .'

He paused, looked at his cigar, and found that it was out.

'Don't light it again,' said Forbes quickly. 'Here, take another.'

Temple laughed.

'The cigars were a present from Rex Bryant,' smiled Sir Graham. 'Sort of a *quid pro quo* in return for an exclusive story. Well, go on, Temple, let's hear how you narrowed down the field.'

Temple eased the band off the cigar.

'Later, when Steve and I made arrangements to go to Aberdeen, and that dreadful accident happened, it became quite obvious that Z.4 was actually at the inn. Only someone staying at the inn could possibly have discovered our arrangements. If any doubt existed in my mind, it was very soon eliminated after our experience at Skerry Lodge.'

Steve shuddered at the recollection.

'Yes,' said Forbes, 'but that didn't eliminate Doctor Steiner or Rex Bryant as possible suspects. Or Iris Archer, too, for that matter. Remember, the whole three of them were staying at the "Royal Gate".'

Temple carefully applied a match to the new cigar.

'If Doctor Steiner had been Z.4 it's hardly likely that he'd have interrupted Iris in her search for the letter,' he argued. 'Don't forget that she was following instructions received from Z.4.'

'You mean through Mrs Moffat? Yes, that's true,' Forbes conceded. 'Now we come to Rex Bryant.'

'Candidly, Sir Graham, I never suspected Rex from the very first,' continued Temple. 'Finding the watch chain on Weston had quite the opposite effect on me from that intended. It more than convinced me of his innocence.'

'Yes,' mused Forbes, 'I rather suspected it was a pretty obvious sort of "plant".'

'And now we come to Mrs Weston,' said Temple. 'Well, in the first place, she was always at the inn, and therefore in a position to overhear most of our conversation; indeed, on one occasion, when we were talking about Lindsay's letter, she actually marched into the room on the pretence of clearing away the coffee things.'

'Seemed natural enough at the time,' commented Forbes.

'Yes, she was a clever little woman, and she had an instinct for time and place,' said Temple. 'Also, as I have already pointed out, she was the most likely person for her husband to confide in about the letter. And thirdly, she made a very bad slip.'

Forbes looked up.

'What do you mean, Temple?'

Paul Temple smiled.

'You probably remember that I discovered certain interesting details about Iris' past. Details which Z.4 knew about, but which Iris was anxious to conceal?'

Forbes nodded. Temple said: 'I received a telegram which confirmed my suspicions about Iris, but when I received the telegram it had already been opened.'

'You mean Mrs Weston actually opened it herself?'

'Precisely. But by mentioning the fact herself, delivering the telegram at a crucial moment, and appearing apparently indifferent to the whole business, the point might very easily have been overlooked.' Temple laughed. 'I told you she had a nice sense of time and place, Sir Graham.'

'I'm beginning to see daylight,' said Forbes. 'As soon as Mrs Weston read that wire, she knew that you knew all there was to know about Iris, and that sooner or later Iris would talk.'

Paul Temple nodded. 'Of course you've guessed the secret, Sir Graham.'

The Chief Commissioner nodded and took a letter from the inside pocket of his overcoat.

'This confirms your theory about Mrs Weston,' he said with a smile. 'Mrs Weston was definitely the chambermaid at the Martinez Hotel. Even in those days the French authorities suspected her of espionage.'

Temple grinned. 'You didn't lose much time checking up, did you, Sir Graham?'

Steve said: 'Paul, you remember when you asked Ernie Weston about your cigarette lighter – what was the idea?'

'Oh, that was only to get his reactions, my dear. I knew then for a certainty that he was in the habit of helping himself to other people's things, and that in all probability he had been responsible for the letter disappearing.'

After he had finished his cigar, Forbes suggested that they should go along to lunch.

When they were seated in the dining car, Temple asked: 'Have you heard anything from the War Office people?'

'Yes, but it was quite hopeless. The chalet was absolutely gutted. Even Hardwick's sketches were just a mass of charred paper.'

During the rest of lunch they discussed general subjects.

Forbes stayed behind for a few minutes in the dining car to finish his liquor, while Temple and Steve returned to their compartment.

'It'll be nice to get home again,' sighed Steve, as she picked up a magazine.

'Presumably that means we'll be off again next week,' grinned her husband.

Steve laughed. 'As a matter of fact, I was thinking of Lake Como. After all, darling, we haven't been there since our honeymoon.'

'Yes,' said Temple, looking thoughtfully out of the window at the wild Northern countryside.

'Do you remember that lake, Paul? The one which was blue – a deep, unforgettable blue?'

'All the lakes were blue, dear,' he smiled.

'I mean the one at the foot of the forest, where we had an argument about fish being able to talk.'

'What an argument!'

'Our first.'

'It was a hell of a row for beginners,' laughed Temple.

Presently Forbes rejoined them, and began speculating once more upon the chances of his paying a visit to America. It was one of his pet topics. Temple and Steve related some of their experiences in the States, and in practically no time they were rushing through the suburbs of London.

As they left the train they saw a massive and familiar figure ahead of them.

'He seems to know his way about, even if he is a foreigner,' commented Steve.

'Why, it's Steiner!' ejaculated Forbes, standing with one foot on the step of a taxi. 'I've a damned good mind to follow him and—'

'Not much point in that, Sir Graham,' Temple assured him, as their own taxi started off.

'But look here, Temple—'

'I see Rex has got his story all right,' said Temple quickly, indicating a newspaper-stand displaying the London *Evening Post*.

'Good old Rex!' applauded Steve, with the genuine reporter's love of a scoop.

'You certainly handed him a first-class story, Sir Graham,' said Temple.

The Chief Commissioner smiled, but he was obviously rather exasperated. 'Now look here, Temple,' he said. 'There's something about all this business I don't quite understand.'

'Oh, and what's that?' asked Temple, and it must be recorded that there was a mischievous twinkle in his eye.

'Well, we know, for instance, who Rex Bryant is,' said Forbes, 'and we know that Iris, van Draper, Guest and Mrs Moffat were members of the organisation. We even know who Z.4 is; but there's still one rather important person we seem to be overlooking!'

'And who's that?'

'Why, the man who came over with you on the *Golden Clipper*,' said Forbes.

Steve nodded. Like the Chief Commissioner, she, too, was obviously perplexed by the identity of the Austrian.

'What on earth was he doing in Scotland?' she asked.

'I think he told us, Steve. He was on holiday.'

'On holiday!' exclaimed Sir Graham, and it must be recorded that he looked very bewildered. 'But who the devil is the fellow?'

Paul Temple smiled. It was a very pleasant smile.

'Believe it or not, Sir Graham,' he said, 'his name is Steiner. Doctor Ludwig Steiner. He is a Professor of Philosophy at the University of Philadelphia.'